5 stars (out of 5) Stephen Maitland-Lewis' *MR. SIMPSON AND OTH-ER SHORT STORIES* include tales that range from droll slice-of-life to high-octane suspense. Maitland-Lewis brings a dry British wit to many of the tales contained in the book. IR Verdict: Stephen Maitland-Lewis wows with *MR. SIMPSON AND OTHER SHORT STORIES*—a triumph of alternative history featuring humor, action, romance and an eclectic mix of characters, genres, and moods—from an exemplary storyteller with a unique voice. **–IndieReader Review**

Stephen Maitland-Lewis, author of the pulse-pounding financial thriller *Duped*, is back with a collection of suspenseful stories that succeed wildly in chronicling the relentless pursuit of success, status, and survival. Prepare to squirm as Maitland-Lewis reveals one dark secret after another. Deliciously ruthless predators rule in this collection of stories about deceit, deception, fraud and power. Highly recommended. **–BestThrillers.com**

LEGACY OF ATONEMENT
An immersive masterful work of alternate history that fans of Phillip K. Dick and Robert Harris will love. **–*BestThrillers.com***

Full of high drama and exciting twists, Legacy of Atonement is a page-turning thriller which reimagines the events from the Second World War and its immediate aftermath. **–*Indie Reader***

This fast-paced thriller has a plethora of unexpected twists and turns that will keep readers guessing to the end. **–*US Review of Books***

The legacy of World War II meets the complexities of the 1950s Cold War in this globe-hopping thriller . . . readers of smart international thrillers will appreciate that the book leaves the door open for further adventures. **–*BookLife* Review**

I0564101

In Maitland-Lewis' thriller sequel to *Legacy of Atonement* (2023), a married couple in Argentina confronts a Nazi conspiracy. This explosive novel is built around an unlikely premise: Given the opportunity, who could pass up capturing a fugitive Adolf Hitler, and his wife, Eva Braun? However, this is exactly what stay-at-home mom Giselle and her husband, Felipe, want to do after a harrowing confrontation with the former dictator at his Paraguayan compound. Now re-established in cosmopolitan Buenos Aires, Giselle and Felipe simply want to live their lives and raise their daughter, even though a plan is apparently in the works to re-establish Hitler and the Nazis. Over the course of this thriller, Maitland-Lewis does an exceptional job of weaving historical details into a narrative that unfolds at a brisk pace within its tightly written framework. Although readers will see a particular cameo coming, they likely won't expect the final twist, which raises an unsettling final question: At what point is it necessary to settle for less than total justice? Aficionados of alternative history and World War II fiction will enjoy pondering such notions. **–*Kirkus Review***

The pursuit of war criminals has never seemed as palpably intense as shown in this exciting work of historical fiction. The hunt for Nazis after the end of World War II has been portrayed in literature (*The Odessa File*), movies (*The Boys from Brazil*), and television (*Hunters*), but intriguingly, this narrative devotes much of its focus to Giselle and the quandary she faces. The horrors that Giselle has seen in this world (i.e., the Holocaust) have impacted her, yet she still believes in the goodness of people. The story benefits from a well-paced plot filled with moments of action and suspense, memorable characters, and a terrific denouement. This novel is sure to generate a buzz among mystery lovers. **–Philip Zozzaro, *US Review of Books***

The Unlikely Huntress is a gripping sequel to author Stephen Maitland-Lewis' *Legacy of Atonement* and continues his international thriller series of espionage, betrayal, and relentless suspense. Original and deftly crafted, *The Unlikely Huntress* continues to showcase Stephen Maitland-Lewis riveting and narrative driven storytelling style making it especially and unreservedly recommended for community library fiction collections. **–*Midwest Book Review***

Giselle and her husband Felipe are two of the few people who know: Hitler and his wife Eva Braun are alive and still in hiding. Trying to balance the unending search with raising their daughter in 1960s Buenos Aires, Giselle stumbles upon an unlikely lead that sends her and her small team of compatriots on a hunt to verify their most dangerous suspicions. Stephen Maitland-Lewis's *The Unlikely Huntress* draws on the real-life stories of Nazi hunters who brought justice to fugitive criminals in the second half of the 20th century. There's a lot to like here, including the setting: a 1960s Buenos Aires where "old-world charm and the embers of revolution" still linger. –**Dan Accardi,** *IndieReader*

5 Stars: If you are looking for a historical espionage thriller flavored with suspense, plot twists, a splash of drama, and action, *The Unlikely Huntress* by Stephen Maitland-Lewis is a great pick. With deliberate prose and vivid depictions, the author transports readers back to 1960s Buenos Aires, Geneva, and Tel Aviv. I gained a clear understanding of the sociopolitical mood and environment during that era. The story unfolds in a way that captures both the characters' day-to-day activities and moments of tension and action, from family moments and events to dangerous outdoor confrontations. The author shows the dangers and high stakes involved in covert operations. –**Keith Mbuya,** *Reader's Favorite*

Tense, atmospheric, and deeply human, *The Unlikely Huntress* is a worthy successor to Legacy of Atonement—and arguably an even richer, more assured work. A great pick for readers who enjoy historical thrillers, slow-burn suspense, and morally complex spy fiction –**Bella Wright,** *Goodreads*

The Unlikely Huntress by Stephen Maitland-Lewis is a superlative Historical Fiction story written with such rich detail it feels incredibly real and in the relevant era. The gorgeous prose, wisdom and clever insight are written on my mind and heart. This is no ordinary novel. If you seek something original, cunning and smart with beautiful depth, this is for you. After finishing *The Unlikely Huntress*, I mulled it over and over and over, loving it more and more by the minute. My connection to it is so strong it feels as though it were written for me! –*Brenda Carleton, NetGalley Review*

Atmospheric and explosive, *The Unlikely Huntress* builds dread in whispers and delivers its punches with startling force. Stephen Maitland-Lewis returns to the harrowing world he built in *Legacy of Atonement* with a powerful sequel, *The Unlikely Huntress*. For those who prize character-driven narratives, *The Unlikely Huntress* is a winner. This is a thriller, yes, but one that understands that fear is often most powerful when it lives in the mind. Tense, atmospheric, and deeply human, *The Unlikely Huntress* is not only a worthy successor to *Legacy of Atonement*. It is also a richer, more mature work that demonstrates Maitland-Lewis' command of suspense and storytelling. A must-read for fans of historical thrillers and morally complex mysteries –*BestThrillers.com*

The Unlikely Huntress by Stephen Maitland-Lewis is the perfect short mystery thriller for any World War II enthusiast. –**Emily Harmon,** *NetGalley Review*

PRAISE FOR STEPHEN MAITLAND-LEWIS'S OTHER TITLES

HERO ON THREE CONTINENTS

A moving, complex and well-crafted fictional biography... Maitland-Lewis renders the multitudinous cast of characters with marvelous detail ... a touching read, with a fictional character to admire. **–Kirkus Reviews**

EMERALDS NEVER FADE

A poignant story of two men whose lives are forever altered by a period of history that should never be forgotten. **–Robert Dugoni**, *NY Times* Bestselling Author

I couldn't put it down until the end. It is a page-turner – greatly enjoyable and informative. Perfecto. **–Connie Martinson**, TV Host of *Connie Martinson Talks Books*

AMBITION

This financial thriller rocks and rolls with sex and skull-duggery and more money than Midas can count. It's un-put-downable. Chilling. **–Kitty Kelley,** seven times *NY Times* Bestselling Biographer

Ambition creates the excitement of free-fall – it's difficult to put down. Who said financial institutions were dull? A wonderful book and a great reading experience. **–Mickey Kantor**, former United States Secretary of Commerce

BOTTICELLI'S BASTARD

Botticelli's Bastard is beautifully written and to its further credit impossible to categorize. Part thriller, part intriguing mystery, this book is compulsive reading. Above all, it is a first-class novel. **–Sir Ronald Harwood,** Oscar® winning writer

Botticelli's Bastard is a fascinating complex and completely compelling novel. It is everything I love, history, art, suspense, intelligence and creativity. I am captivated. **–M.J. Rose**, International Bestselling Author

My interest in collecting important art came together with my love of thrillers. Stephen Maitland-Lewis' *Botticelli's Bastard* is a great read. **–Arnold Kopelson,** Oscar® and Golden Globe® winning producer

PRAISE FOR STEPHEN MAITLAND-LEWIS'S OTHER TITLES

DUPED

A realistic and engagingly descriptive novel. —**Kirkus Reviews**

DUPED delivers the excitement of a heist film with the exotic adventure of a globetrotting spy tale. While Maitland-Lewis' dialogue-driven writing makes for fast-reading, well-crafted adventures through portions of Africa, Europe and California will please the travel-starved masses. —**BestThrillers.com**

In *DUPED*, author Stephen Maitland-Lewis has written a novel of high-stake schemes, suspense and sex. A deftly crafted, impressively original, and inherently riveting read from first page to last. —**Midwest Book Review**

Stephen Maitland-Lewis has secured his place as a supremely gifted writer of the cunning, courage and evil residing within the human spirit. With his special talent of developing characters capable of both heroic and treacherous acts, Maitland-Lewis relies on his wits to create another fabulous book. *DUPED* ranks as another masterpiece from this writer with a hugely impressive body of work. —**Jim Engster**, President Louisiana Radio Network

Maitland-Lewis delivers a sophisticated, high-stakes, international thriller that will make you grateful for the life you have, providing you aren't already caught in a web of corruption and deceit in the sweltering Nigerian streets. Be thankful you're a reader and not a character in this haunting tale of desperation, greed and power. —**Stephen Jay Schwartz**, *LA Times* bestselling author

MR. SIMPSON AND OTHER SHORT STORIES

Personal connections, and our failure to make and tend to them, dominate this entrancing collection of irony-infused short stories, set mostly in postwar Europe and America. The greatest lure of the stories are the characters. Maitland-Lewis (*Botticelli's Bastard*) sharply limns the foibles of the well-heeled and privileged. The decisions Maitland-Lewis's characters make haunt them forever, and the characters themselves will haunt the readers. Takeaway: The community of characters—the good, the desperate, the greedy—will grab readers' hearts and make them care, story after story. Great for fans of: Graham Swift, Julian Barnes —**BookLife** - *Publisher's Weekly*

THE
Unlikely
HUNTRESS

THE
Unlikely
HUNTRESS

STEPHEN
MAITLAND-LEWIS

Hildebrand Books

an imprint of W. Brand Publishing

NASHVILLE, TENNESSEE

HILDE
BRAND
BOOKS

Hildebrand Books an imprint of W. Brand Publishing
j.brand@wbrandpub.com
www.wbrandpub.com

Cover design by designchik.net
Author Photo by Darien Photographic

The Unlikely Huntress – Stephen Maitland-Lewis first edition

Available in Hardcover, Paperback, Kindle, and eBook formats.
Hardcover ISBN: 979-8-89503-032-5
Paperback ISBN: 979-8-89503-020-2
eBook ISBN: 979-8-89503-021-9

Release date: December 2, 2025
Library of Congress Control Number: 2025917081

CONTENTS

for Darien
with love

CHAPTER ONE

G iselle chased her daughter, ducking and twisting through a sea of Elena's friends' parents, all dressed casually in formal greys, beiges, and creams. She finally caught up and hooked her arm around the little girl's middle, swung her back, and then lifted her into a two-armed squeeze snug against her chest. Elena's breathing slowed—heart beating fast as a hummingbird's from her mad dash through the party guests—and her dark, wild eyes focused on her mother. Giselle said to her in the low tone of secret-telling, "It's time."

"Time?" Elena repeated at full volume, as though she were trying to be heard over fireworks or an airplane's overhead roar.

The girl was always high energy; it seemed every other day that she wore Giselle and Felipe's energy down to a nub. Giselle often narrowly convinced herself to take a shower and brush her teeth before her head hit the pillow, her exhausted limbs luxuriating under the downy comforter—a wedding gift from her cousin Anna that embraced her and her husband. She knew Felipe was every bit as tired as she was, but so frequently his eyes trained on the ceiling, his stare interrupted only by slow, introspective blinks.

"Time for presents?" Elena clarified, though she already knew what *time* meant. She knew by the mischievous glint in her mother's eyes.

The newly four-year-old girl was quite adroit in most cases when it came to pronouncing words—a precocious reader known to fling herself on her father's lap while he sat expressionless at the dinner table reading the newspaper, occasionally shaking his head. Elena would beg him to listen to her read the latest book Giselle bought her. In its infancy, this practice involved asking Felipe to read to *her*. Both Felipe and Giselle had been so proud, yet mildly sad the way parents can feel at the fading of a childhood stage they'd learned to treasure—when Elena switched to asking to read the story herself. Giselle's heart always warmed watching Felipe gently correct the little girl's mispronunciations; she credited his loving, unintrusive teaching style with the fact that Elena seemed to experience no anxiety as a young reader. She progressed more each day, from a child's clumsy diction to a style of reading and talking quite sophisticated for her age.

Even as she marveled at it, Giselle secretly experienced blips of euphoria at the words which her daughter was apt to pack with extra w's. For instance, "presents" still came out sounding like "pwesents."

As soon as Giselle set her down, Elena zipped toward the extended folding table at the head of the community hall they'd rented for her birthday. The table was draped with a faint peach-colored plastic tablecloth, and a pink "Happy Birthday" banner repeated at intervals across it. Under each arched banner were pink and blue gifts of every kind: a blue present, a striped, pink ball, a blue hat the conductor of a marching band might wear, and a pink lady's hat with long ribbons trailing from it. Elena had squealed with glee when she'd seen it.

She wasn't a materialistic girl. It wasn't even so much that she was thrilled about the pile of presents on the table or the prospect of opening them in front of her friends, some of whom Elena acquired from the park Giselle had been taking her to more often lately. The same park where Giselle could get lost in a daze watching children pump their legs on the swings, and their mothers, a handful of them heavy with second or third pregnancies, assist with soft pushes from behind.

But there was a particular present Elena had her heart set on, one she mentioned breathlessly in, it seemed, every conversation with her parents that was not about what was for dinner or what book she and Giselle would pick out next.

It was a board game released a few years prior but new to Elena, called *Risk*.

When her parents first heard this was what she most wanted for her birthday, they were surprised. Giselle remembered the scene clearly: they had been sitting around the table for a dinner of plump humita empanadas, which Felipe was washing down with a cold beer. Giselle had heard of the game before, but Felipe wasn't much for keeping up with culture outside of which countries were boiling with tensions and coming close to threatening war.

Knowing the look of the game, that it was a layout of the globe with the continents shown in different, vibrant colors, Giselle asked, "Do you think you actually want a map instead, sweetheart?" The girl had been known to excitedly spin around the sepia-colored globe in her father's office from time to time, stopping its frenzied rotation with one of her little fingers and trying to name the country she was pointing to.

"*No*," Elena said, somewhat indignant. "It's not just a map, Mommy. You take lands." Giselle and Felipe had exchanged amused glances. "It's good to get Australia first because it's small." No sooner had she said it than her eyes went wide, and her hand clamped over her mouth as she realized she'd given away a hint to winning the game to the very opponents she'd probably play against. They both smiled, holding back laughs.

"But, Elena, how many people does it take to play?" her mother asked.

"Just two." *Tw-oo*. "Me and you could play, Daddy."

Giselle wasn't offended by this in the least, nor had she been any of the times Elena chose to pounce on her father's lap for reading time. She was a Daddy's girl through and through, and Giselle loved to see it. It confirmed for her all over again that her heart had been right to leap at Felipe's attentions back when they were starting their courtship in the midst of an international meltdown.

"Sounds like it's a game of strategy," Felipe said.

Elena nodded enthusiastically. Then she said it. "Like in the military. You get conta–" She stopped and looked at Giselle for help with the word.

"Con-ti-nents," Giselle enunciated, distracted and carefully watching her husband's expression for his reaction.

"Con-ti-nents," Elena repeated. "But if I get Australia, maybe you could get Germany, Daddy."

Giselle had seen the subtle shift in Felipe's eyes, the gleam present whenever he interacted with his daughter was replaced with dullness, a muffled misery at the sound of its name. Still looking at him, trying with her gaze to offer him some comfort, Giselle said, "Germany's a country, honey, not a continent."

They both questioned her excitement for the game, but she couldn't be dissuaded by the 10+ age rating or that the game apparently could take eight hours in some cases. This only excited her more: *all day* playing *military* with Daddy.

Elena rushed past the other long table in the room which was draped with a matching tablecloth. A dazzling assortment of food meant to satisfy the tastebuds of Elena's friends and their parents sat on top: delicious, crisp chorizo empanadas, salad with roasted nori, Neapolitan-style pizza the kids had gone wild for, ricotta tarts with sourdough crust, dulce de leche for the adults, and fructose del bosque ice cream for the children. Though the servings were well picked over now, Elena, in her excitement, had hardly eaten a thing.

Giselle made sure to instruct Elena to be gracious about every gift she received, to look the gift giver in the eyes and thank them by name. Still, she took a seat next to her daughter on the off chance that if Elena forgot her manners, Giselle could remind her.

Thankfully, Elena was perfectly behaved as she slowly tore apart the paper on each gift, saying, "Thank you *so* much," to each child seated in a semicircle on the thinly carpeted floor in front of her. Patient politeness was easier for her because early in the pile she opened her present from her parents and found the game of *Risk* she'd been holding her breath for.

After that, she received a stand-up doll with a blonde bob cut that talked, which came from her playground friend Joey, who blushed beet-red when she thanked him *so* much. Elena opened another doll with a putty-like face, so ugly one had to find it cute, with long red hair that stood on end. Giselle had never seen anything like it but assumed her daughter had, and had wanted one, from its ecstatic reception. A doll called Barbie with thick eyelashes and curly bangs.

Finally, she got to the present from Charlene, the little girl who'd arguably become Elena's best friend. The two of them were able to spend hours contentedly playing pretend together on the gentle knolls of the playground. Giselle had been concerned Charlene wouldn't make it—to Elena's vast disappointment—they had not seen Charlene at the playground for several days.

As Elena tore the paper off the oblong package that signaled another board game, Charlene, a freckled auburn-haired girl in a blue gingham dress, couldn't contain her enthusiasm: "It stands up!" she shouted.

Intently curious to find out what her dear friend meant, Elena set up the board game on the spot for all to witness. She was delighted to discover the three-dimensional structure that included rickety stairs and a basin-looking thing and what appeared to be a laundry basket suspended upside down. It was called *Mousetrap*, and Elena and Charlene set to playing it at once. Charlene had accomplished what only a best friend could: choosing a present that made the one Elena had petitioned for through the preceding months pale in comparison.

Shaking her head with a smile, Giselle set off in search of Charlene's mother, one of those heavily pregnant women she always saw pushing a swing at the playground, to thank her for her part in the gift selection. However, Giselle couldn't find Marcia anywhere. She'd circled her way back to the front of the room when a woman with long brown hair and a strong jaw, perhaps a couple years younger than Giselle, approached with a friendly smile.

"Hi, you look a little lost. Are you looking for Charlene's mom?"

Giselle nodded hesitantly.

"Thought you might be," the young woman said. Registering Giselle's confusion, she stuck her hand out. "Sorry, I'm Karen. I'm Charlene's nanny."

Giselle appreciated her handshake, warm but firm with confidence. "I wasn't aware Charlene had a nanny. I've always seen her with her mother at the playground."

Karen sneaked a happy wave to Charlene, who'd surfaced from the game long enough to make eye contact with her. "Oh, I'm brand new. Just hired a couple weeks ago when Marcia went into labor."

Giselle could feel her mouth hanging open. She didn't know why this caught her off guard, why she reacted so strongly to such an expected event. She shook her head a little as though to help the news settle in.

"I suppose I should have anticipated that. The last time I saw her she'd looked as if she were due any day now. I was coming to thank her for the amazing gift—Elena's enchanted by it—but I guess I'll have to include that in the congratulations card."

Karen smiled and tilted her head conspiratorially toward Giselle. "Congratulate away, but between you and me, I had a hand in the present-picking."

"No kidding."

"I'm so glad it wasn't a flop. This is my first real outing with her among her peers. Imagine if I'd tanked my first important nanny duty by picking a terrible gift." Karen swiped her hand in an exaggerated gesture of relief across her forehead.

Giselle couldn't help but laugh. "You couldn't have done a better job. I'm amazed at the—"

"The 3D structure?" Karen interrupted. "How it's almost like monkey bars or something on top of a game board?"

"Exactly."

"Oh, they're coming out with so many exciting things in the world of toys."

"They are," Giselle acknowledged, eyeing the pile of opened presents beside Elena and Charlene, and the circle of onlookers around them who'd taken to cheering on one girl and then the other. "To tell you the truth, I'm not too excited about this Barbie doll business."

Karen rolled her eyes in agreement. "Waist the size of a pencil, and that sour face. Are you kidding?"

Giselle laughed. She hadn't exactly been a social butterfly in recent months. Most of her excursions were to the playground or the grocery store, but still, it had been a long time since she'd met a person she could get along with so quickly. And with Felipe being . . . well, the way Felipe had been for quite a long time now, she felt hungry for a friend.

"I'm happy for Marcia," Giselle said, hoping to keep the conversation flowing.

"God, me too," Karen said. "But I'm jealous too, you know."

"Eager to have one yourself?"

"I can-*not* wait," Karen emphasized. "It's why I'm nanny. I love the hell out of kids. Just got to get through the other stuff first—get engaged, marry the guy, all of that."

Giselle enjoyed a hearty laugh, the kind that makes your head tilt back and then drop back down heavily. "So, is there a guy?"

"Yes. And he's a prince, really. And we're coming up on it, marriage I mean. He's trying to act nonchalant, but I know he's itching to propose. His name is Hans."

Giselle couldn't keep the edges of her smile from wavering at this last note of Karen's disclosure. *Hans.* It was a German name if ever she'd heard one. Even now, years after she, Felipe, and her uncle Daniel had infiltrated Hitler's secret compound in Paraguay and almost succeeded in capturing him along with his presumed-dead wife, Eva Braun, Giselle had to remind herself that not all Germans were on his side. Not all Germans were Nazis or Nazi sympathizers. In fact, a too-small number rebelled, to their credit, against the regime.

She took a deep breath and returned to smiling. "Well, if you're as good a mother as you are a nanny to Charlene, you'll be great."

"I can only hope." Karen's eyes lingered on Giselle's face, noticing a wistful pall lined with some sadness that descended every time she spoke of babies, of mothering.

"What about you?" she asked, nudging Giselle gently with her elbow. "Think you'd want another?"

Mulling over how to answer the question, Giselle flashed back to approximately this time last year, somewhere around Elena's third birthday, when Giselle had asked Felipe the same question. The birthday party had been smaller, and Elena had been more interested in balloons and cake than presents, but the hullabaloo had been just as intoxicating then. Giselle couldn't stop thinking after the party about how, even through being exhausted, she felt elated from giving her daughter such a magical experience. It rivaled freeing the young children from Hitler's evil medical experiments for the most fulfilled and rewarded she had ever felt. She couldn't help but think what a good big sister three-year-old Elena would make.

"I would love another one," she answered honestly. "I never dreamed I could love someone the way I love Elena."

"Well . . ." Karen left the word hanging, the question mark behind it implied. Why *didn't* she go ahead and have another? She already had the man, the marriage.

Giselle's eyes found Felipe through the crowd as though he had a strong magnetic pull on her. He stood behind the ravaged food table, putting what was left from the fragrant dishes into containers before the party was even over. She noticed he had already cleared most of the table, leaving only Elena's birthday cake, a layer of white frosting under pink and blue lattice work. Elena had loved these two colors from the time she could first pronounce color names. During art time with Giselle, she loved to see the two paints mixed into a deep cotton candy-like swirl.

Right now, Felipe seemed immune to the cake's charms, physically and emotionally taxed by the prospect of interacting with the other parents.

Even if she wanted to, there was no way Giselle could deny the truth when it looked her right in the face: Felipe was suffering from depression.

Ever since Elena's birth, Felipe—in his preoccupation with making good on his promise to track down Hitler and bring him to justice—had gone from determined to despondent. He frequently told her how, now that he had Elena to worry about, he couldn't help but obsess all the more about the children kept captive and harmed in Hitler's terrible Paraguayan compound. Before Elena came along, he seemed to have a bottomless store of resilience to take the dead-ends and red herrings of his search in stride. After he looked his baby daughter in her dark doe eyes, though, he started absorbing the fact that he hadn't been able to ensnare the world's most notorious and wicked fugitive, as a personal failing as a father. He seemed to grow ever more convinced that a world with Hitler at large, spreading his violent prejudice—just as a factory fills the air with polluting clouds of smoke—was a world unspeakably unsafe and not good enough for his little daughter.

Giselle knew that until the monster had been put away for good, Felipe would continue to feel the world was too dangerous for Elena and would never agree to a second child. But of course, she couldn't say any of this to Karen, no matter how much she trusted her, or how surprisingly close she felt to the young nanny.

Giselle tried to strike just the right blend of truth and necessary privacy-keeping. "Well, we always talked about having at least two, and I'm ready . . ."

"But your husband's not?" Karen followed Giselle's eyes to the man with the downcast eyes dusting crumbs off the buffet table.

"He's been feeling down," Giselle offered by way of explanation. "I don't think we'll be ready until he's in a better place."

"Mind if I offer a word of advice?" Karen ventured.

Giselle looked surprised but said, "Sure."

"How much alone time have you two had since Elena came along?"

Giselle admitted it hadn't been much. She'd been fortunate to stay home with Elena and attend to her needs full-time. Their little family was comfortable but not so financially comfortable that they could have afforded a nanny, even if they'd wanted to. Still, if Felipe hadn't appeared growingly unenthusiastic about the pleasures of a night out with his wife, they could have called babysitters to allow them time for a date on occasion.

Karen shrugged as her way of emphasizing the obvious. "Initiate a date night yourself. *Insist.* Get him out on the town and then, you know, out to a nice hotel or something—away from the pattering of little feet, precious as they are."

Giselle blushed furiously and laughed, but she also took her new friend's words to heart. "I don't suppose you'd—"

How quickly Karen had picked up the ability to finish Giselle's sentences. "—babysit Elena so you can get your fella in the mood? I would love to. Let me write down my information for you."

No sooner had Karen scrawled her contact details on the back of a party napkin than Charlene came running at them full throttle, bouncing up and down, requesting that Karen join them in the next round of *Mousetrap.* After smiling and waving goodbye, Giselle unfolded the napkin and saw Karen's telephone number along with her full name written inside.

Feeling her eyebrows knit together, Giselle looked at her husband, who seemed to feel her gaze this time. He looked back at her, questioningly.

~~~

In his Geneva office, pacing as far as the spiraled cord on his phone would allow, Daniel Lavy irritably switched over from his current call to the other line. Someone had been calling over and over, not taking the hint that he was busy.

He offered the caller an irritated "What?" in place of a professional "Hello."

"Daniel, it's me. Felipe."

Happy as Daniel normally would have been to hear from his old friend and nephew by marriage, he hadn't yet shaken off his soreness from not being allowed to complete his telephone conversation.

"Felipe, it's always good to hear from you, but this better be damned good if you're calling every five seconds. I was on the phone, you know. There are important things that need my attention sometimes," Daniel said sharply.

"I was just discussing how the price of gold is hovering at $35.35 right now. I'm thinking about switching to silver. It's holding steady at a dollar per ounce. Now, there's clearly a greater potential for profit there, so as I said, I'm thinking about switching," he rambled. "Do *you* have opinions on that? Or do you want to let me get back to my call so I can discuss this properly with somebody who knows something about silver and gold?"

On the other end of the line, Felipe listened to Daniel's grousing with a smile. Daniel Lavy was famously grouchy when interrupted or inconvenienced, to talk to the man before he'd had his breakfast and coffee in the morning was to address a scowling stone wall. Hearing Daniel's voice would have had the counterintuitive effect of brightening Felipe's mood even in the throes of his depression. But today was a new day for Felipe.

For the first time in too many months, he felt energy pumping through his veins. It meant he was ready to take anything Daniel could dish out—not to mention amused to hear what a sharp left turn the man's tone was about to take.

"Are you done now?" Felipe asked.

"Why this goddamned urgency? Is my niece okay? Is Elena? Because if they are, then I don't know why—"

"They're both fine. And so am I, thank you for asking," Felipe said with a teasing tone. Then he could hold back no longer. "Daniel, I think I've got a lead."

"Concerning—"

"Concerning how we find Hitler."

Daniel's concern with the competing values of silver and gold instantly subsided. When the other line blinked red for his attention, he switched over to it long enough to hang up on the caller.

Switching back to Felipe, he sat down and leaned back in his rolling leather office chair.

"Back up," Daniel said. "Tell me everything."

CHAPTER TWO

It had happened the night he was supposed to go out to the dinner Giselle had been planning for the two of them since Elena's birthday party. Anticipating any objection, he might come up with, she'd accommodated his dislike of multi-course dinners in restaurants that made every tourist's list of places to visit in Buenos Aires. Instead, she chose a bistro where he could have one of the stacked pretzeled sandwiches he loved, and they could share ricotta cake, maybe with some delightfully rich sabayon ice cream for dessert.

Felipe had been sitting on the bed they shared, restless lately with his wife, when he heard the cloth-muffled thump of her setting her purse on the countertop, the chime of its various contents knocking together. She wasn't normally impatient with him. This would be her only way of asking him to, for the love of God, hurry up.

"This isn't what I meant by tell me everything!" Daniel bellowed. He wasn't nearly as patient as Giselle. The sound of his crystal tumbler landing heavily on his mahogany desk near the phone—ripping off the distinctive slosh and the rattle of the sparse "rocks" he liked in his whiskey—Felipe knew he needed to skim the narrative.

Felipe wasn't normally such a long-winded storyteller, but scenes from this night flashed so vividly in his working memory.

He thought about but certainly did not drag Daniel through how he'd sat staring down an errant black mark on the bedroom wall until it lost all meaning. This should have been wonderful, he knew: a night out filled with fine bistro selections with the love of his life, but he could hardly muster a polite smile to match her eagerness.

How he had mustered the impossible strength to push himself up from the bed and join his wife in the kitchen. How Elena had barreled toward him with locomotive strength and speed, leaping in his arms as she chanted, "Daddy, don't leave. No babysitter. Stay, stay, stay, stay."

How solicitously Giselle had spoken, leaning her forehead against Elena's as she reminded her how much she'd liked Karen at her birthday party. "Charlene loves her. Can you imagine not loving someone Charlene loves?"

How, setting Elena down, Felipe had reassured her that Karen had the phone number of the restaurant where they would be, and that Mummy and Daddy would be home *the moment* they finished eating. Giselle's unintentional sigh was a gentle breeze against Felipe's increasingly storm-like pace of breath. He was vaguely aware of speaking with an intensity disproportionate to a little girl's resistance to being babysat, but in a way, he could do nothing about it. Just like Giselle, he could observe the overbearing father looking deep in his daughter's eyes, clutching her spindly arms in his palms, and swearing to her, "Daddy would never put you in an unsafe situation. Do you understand? There's nothing more important in the world to me than you knowing you are secure. In fact, maybe we should resc—"

"Elena!" Giselle broke in, inverting her frustration into a tone of excitement. "Why don't you pick out some of your favorite animal toys to show Miss Karen? I think she'd love to know what you've named them and where you got them from."

Whether genuinely excited in her own right or eager to disengage from this strange intensity she had unlocked in her father, Elena skittered away toward her bedroom.

Before Giselle could voice her objection to his truncated attempt to change their plans, Felipe pled his defense: "I'm her father, Giselle. I must make certain she knows she is safe. If I don't . . ."

"Felipe!" Giselle cried in a voice laced with empathy. "My love, it's one night. Set down this heavy burden you carry just for that long. Elena will be fine. And you and I deserve one night away, just the two of us."

Gazing at her husband's unconvinced face, Giselle suddenly brightened, a lightbulb flickering on in her mind. "I know what will help." She fished in her purse for the folded slip of paper. "She lives very close—she probably hasn't left yet. Let's give her a call. I know you'll feel better—"

This part, Felipe did tell Daniel in some detail. How he'd been unable to hear anything else she said.

To Daniel, Felipe repeated the name from the slip.

"Fegel?" Even this much caused a hitch of suspicion in Daniel's voice.

"And behind the *l* a small squiggle. As though—"

"She started to write another letter." In his office, Daniel stood up with such speed and carelessness that it knocked his tumbler sideways. The watery remains of his whiskey bled across the dark wood.

"Could you tell what letter it was going to be?" Daniel nearly shouted, as if he was repeating the question for a second or third time.

At last, Felipe smiled. Relaxed. Felt he could breathe for the first time in a long time.

"Yes. It looked like she started to write *e*."

~~~

Former architect Simon Wiesenthal had survived more in about three and half years than most people could imagine surviving in their worst nightmares: the Janowska, Kraków-

Plaszow, and Gross-Rosen concentration camps followed by a death march to Chemnitz, Buchenwald, and the Mauthausen concentration camp, finally put to a merciful end in May 1945.

Two short but interminable years later, Wiesenthal founded a sort of document storehouse in Linz, where anyone could contribute information, they believed was beneficial to the prosecuting of war crimes. Then, only three years ago, he opened another similar center in Vienna. In addition to being known for his tireless and humanitarian efforts to help Jewish refugees locate missing family members, Wiesenthal became known to many—and a personal hero to Felipe—when he played a part in the Mossad's capture of Adolf Eichmann, a crooked-faced SS officer who had played one of the major parts in organizing the Holocaust, also known as "The Final Solution."

Daniel remembered the night Eichmann was taken down, primarily because an elated Felipe had called him, his voice alive with optimism.

"We're getting somewhere!" Felipe shouted in Daniel's ear, making him jerk the receiver away with a wince. He had interrupted Daniel in the course of watching a Primera División match and downing a single malt scotch. Still, Daniel couldn't help but smile. Felipe talked about Wiesenthal and his co-Nazi hunters the way other men would have talked about soccer teams chasing a painfully white ball down the too-green field on television: as though they were all, indeed, teammates.

"This is good news, Daniel!" Felipe said with playful defensiveness when his uncle-in-law laughed.

"It's wonderful news, Felipe." Daniel had laughed only because it struck him exactly why Felipe felt so exuberant about this capture—why he called Daniel in the middle of a game to gush about Wiesenthal and his thinking man's approach to Nazi hunting. "How *is* that baby girl of yours?"

"She's perfect, perfect." Felipe had developed this linguistic tic when discussing his bundle of joy: listing her positive attributes twice, as though once just wasn't enough. She was so strong, marvelously strong—as demonstrated by the fact that she could already grip Felipe's finger. She was such a happy, happy baby, evidenced by her smiles that Felipe was certain were not just gas, the way that her pediatrician may have claimed. If Felipe had been a hellbent fighter before, since the arrival of baby Elena, he had become relentless.

With a passing bitterness he swallowed along with the mostly melted cubes left in his glass, Daniel thought of his own reasons for acting relentlessly against the shithead Nazi enemy. He thought of losing his mother and father, his younger sister. What tonight might have been like if he could've enjoyed the football match with them—as opposed to watching in hopes of avoiding the still-staggering undeniable pain of their loss.

He would've envied this daring young warrior who'd married his niece if Daniel himself didn't find fresh motivation in fighting the good fight from the same source as Felipe: Giselle, Elena, and yes, Felipe too. *Family.* Ever since the day his long-lost niece had shown up on his doorstep hoping for his help, he had regained a sense of family he'd once assumed was gone forever.

If not surprised, Daniel was pleased that, when he suggested giving Wiesenthal a call, Felipe said he already had.

"And?" This seemed to be Daniel's catchword for their conversation.

"He thinks that what we're both thinking is possible."

Daniel put the tacit into words: "That Karen Fegel is actually Karen Fegelein."

If their theory was correct, it meant that this Karen Fegel whom Giselle had befriended at a birthday party was none other than the daughter of Hermann Fegelein—commander in the Nazi combat branch known as Waffen-SS—and Gretl Braun, the sister of Eva Braun, and therefore Hitler's sister-in-law. Fegelein, whom Daniel had never not referred to as "that smug-faced Nazi scum," was one of the most notorious SS officers, responsible for the murder of thousands. Adding to his ignoble reputation was the fact that, by virtue of the marital relationship, he was considered among Hitler's *elite entourage.*

The simpering opportunist had been shot for desertion—"May he rot in hell!" Daniel put in—but it now seemed possible that Fegelein's widow and little daughter had escaped from the Paraguayan compound before Felipe and Daniel had landed there with the U.S. Marines.

"Do you think Gretl might still be alive?" Felipe asked.

"No reason to think they wouldn't have escaped together. If this is indeed the daughter, I wouldn't be surprised if the mother's around."

"And do you think it's possible?" Felipe started, his voice climbing in excitement. "That maybe she's the one to lead us to her Aunt Eva and Uncle Adolf?"

Daniel had just begun answering in the affirmative when Felipe, buckled by a thought that churned his stomach, said, "Dear God, Daniel. To think of her being around all those children . . ."

Knowing this topic could send Felipe into a full spiral, Daniel said, "This woman is a goldmine, our biggest break so far. Concentrate on that. Clearly, she can't be alone with Elena."

"No!" Felipe sounded horrified.

"But we must keep her close." Absentmindedly, Daniel mopped the pale amber spill on his desk with the sleeve of his suit jacket.

"Without tipping her off," Felipe moaned in agreement. "What do you think, Daniel? What do I do?"

~~~

"The first step is mastering your grip on the racquet," Joaquin explained to the two rapt little faces turned up at him. Demonstrating on his own adult-sized racquet, the lanky tennis instructor—whose foppish curls and bright eyes made him look more like a teenager than the twenty-something man he was—fixed his hinge-like grip at an angle near the head. "Try on your own about here."

Playing twins for the day, Charlene and Elena both wore white pleated skirts that resembled daisies when they twirled, which they did frequently on the chalk-dusted, navy tennis court. Just then, Elena twirled so fast—chasing her racquet in a wild arc around her body—that she crashed onto her bottom.

As quickly as she did, Giselle was on her feet. But before she could rush to the court and scoop Elena up, Karen caught her elbow. "Giselle, Giselle, Giselle." It was the only way Karen reminded her of Felipe: he doubled his adjectives, especially when it concerned Elena. Similarly, Karen often tripled words, especially names. How many times on these playdates had Giselle heard Karen say, "Charlene, Charlene, Charlene, it is time to go, my bug," or, eliciting more giggles still, "Charlene, Charlene, Charlene—what am I going to do with you?"

Having Giselle's attention times three, Karen explained, "She's going to be just fine, I promise you. Watch what happens." She nodded toward the court just as Elena bounced back to her feet. It would even seem that she'd found the fall somewhat delightful, as she cackled and immediately lurched into her wild swing a second time.

"These are clay courts," Karen explained. "They give you a decently high bounce still, but they slow things down a little and aren't as hard on falls as asphalt." Answering Giselle's mildly astonished look, Karen explained, "I looked into it."

Giselle still found herself struggling with moments like these. When Karen would seem so remarkably . . . human— the antithesis of a Nazi monster—that Giselle would find herself thinking, *We don't* know *that she's a Fegelein. Maybe that squiggle was every bit as innocent as she'd first insisted to Felipe.* In moments like this, she was tempted to simply think, *Of course she looked into it—she's an excellent nanny,* and leave it at that.

Joaquin reeled his racquet from the front of his body just slightly behind his shoulder-line, telling the girls, "We will start with a short backswing—what I'm doing. Bring your racquets back just like this." He demonstrated the wind-up and then brought the racquet forward with an efficient slice.

"And then we have the follow-through. Practice just like this." He demonstrated several more times. "Then we can work on bringing our grip on the handle down slowly, lengthening the backstroke slowly. This way we don't do as Elena and—"

Rather than supplying words, Joaquin swung his own racquet maniacally as the little girl had done, going so far as to fall on his rear end. This sent both girls into paroxysms of giggles.

"Lord, he's adorable," Karen said before Giselle had a chance to basically say the same thing.

"He's so kind with the kids."

"Yeah, that too." While Giselle laughed—an honest laugh, the kind she found hard to hold back when the two were on the sidelines of whatever activity they'd arranged for Elena and Charlene, Karen said, "No, seriously, he's great with the kids. I'm so glad this club has an instructor just for children."

Across the course of several of these set-ups, Giselle had grown to know Karen reasonably well. She hadn't given her mother's name, but she had confirmed that her mother was still living here in Buenos Aires. Giselle also learned that Karen had lived in Buenos Aires as a child but moved away for a while before she and her mother returned. When she lined the facts up like this, Giselle felt much less persuaded of Karen's innocence, no matter how innocuous, even quaint, her personality made her seem. Giselle felt certain, for instance, that when Karen had "moved away," she was in Paraguay—but it wasn't a topic Karen liked to discuss. And Giselle knew she dared not push too hard lest she raise suspicions.

Now, however, Giselle sensed a topic where she could dig in a little. And she needed to; she was getting nowhere fast, and she couldn't keep pretending that Elena—cartwheeling, chatty, active little Elena—was too shy to need a nanny forever. That's how this had all been set up: a way for Elena to get more and more accustomed to Karen with her mother still present. This worked better in Giselle's mind than simply saying she wanted the girls to go on playdates, but she was no longer interested in dating her own husband, thereby needing a sitter.

Giselle took a long sip of her still water. "I certainly wish I'd had an instructor like him growing up. I liked tennis all right as it was, but I can't help but think I might have loved it." When Karen didn't immediately respond, Giselle prodded gently. "Did you ever play when you were growing up?"

Karen just shook her head, smiling spontaneously when Charlene took the sort of swing with her racquet one is meant to take with a baseball bat, and she inadvertently sent it flying.

"How about where you lived in between your times in Buenos Aires?" Giselle dared to ask. "Where did you say that was?"

Here was another quality that tended to make Giselle suspicious of Karen: she knew how to dodge questions deftly.

"There was definitely no tennis there. Well, none that wasn't so ridiculously competitive it sucked the fun right out. God did I hate that place."

Just as Giselle was swallowing her disappointment with another dead end, Karen continued. "Well . . . I hated *most* of it. There was a guy."

"Now, as long as the swing is feeling comfortable, try your hand just a little lower on the handle," Joaquin said. "Try swinging it back and forth with your wrist first, see how that feels."

Giselle allowed her eyes to glitter. "What *guy*?"

"Wolfgang," Karen said almost dreamily, "a young German soldier I dated for . . . those years."

Here was an example of where the internal friction overtook Giselle. Because of how much she enjoyed spending time with Karen, she was tempted to argue that not all German soldiers were SS, and this "Wolfgang" could have been a perfectly honorable man. On the other hand, her skin crawled at his name and job, specifically *"soldier."*

"A serious boyfriend?" she asked.

"Now!" Joaquin whooped. "We try with the ball." He held aloft the tennis ball, which glowed like a seashell at noon. He might as well have announced cake and ice cream. The girls literally leapt up and down in excitement.

"Very," Karen emphasized. "Don't get me wrong, Hans is wonderful. But when we're talking about marriage and family, I can't help but think of Wolfgang sometimes. I once dreamed of having a family with him, too."

When Karen mentioned that they'd broken up "suddenly" in 1959, Giselle couldn't help but speculate that their disunion could have conveniently stemmed from Wolfgang getting left behind by Hitler's entourage that escaped from Paraguay.

"But he was pretty wonderful, too." Karen smiled a faraway smile.

I'll bet he was, Giselle thought, her internal voice now saturated in bitterness. Apparently, some of it showed through her mask of civility, because Karen shook her head in remorse.

"Giselle, Giselle, Giselle. Forgive me for blundering on like this about marriage and family. I've got baby fever right now, but I didn't mean . . ."

. . . *to bring up the fact that your husband is too depressed about not finding Hitler to try for baby number two,* Giselle thought, filling in blanks of Karen's unfinished sentence. Giselle quickly waved off Karen's concerns. And she tried to think fast. The last thing she needed was to derail Karen from talking about her ex-boyfriend. Giselle didn't know what she would discover by tugging on this thread, but it felt promising.

"Please, no worries. If there was a look that crossed my face, I was just thinking about my own ex-boyfriend, before Felipe. God knows am I glad I didn't have a family with him."

"He was no Felipe, huh?"

"No," Giselle said, thinking almost faster than she herself could keep up with.

"He was . . . selfish and unmotivated. Something of a coward, now that I really think about it. He was a bad boyfriend and would've made a poor father."

Karen tilted her head. On the court, Elena's racquet slapped the tennis ball within inches of the net. As much as Giselle was tempted to cheer and shout her name, she couldn't allow Karen to get sidetracked now. She could tell Karen was taking her bait.

"Then why on earth did you date him? I know I haven't known you that long, Giselle, but sticking with a loser doesn't seem like your style."

"Well . . ." Giselle pretended to find words for some delicate truth about her not-at-all-made-up disaster of a boyfriend before Felipe. "What God did not give him in the personality department,"—her hand drew a circle around her face—"he made up for here."

"Ah! So, he was easy on the eyes."

"Oh, Felipe is too. It's just that with Felipe I get the whole package—looks and a good man. Is that . . ." She swallowed the bile rising in her throat.

"Is that what you got with Wolfgang, also? I know you've said he was a . . . wonderful man . . ." She tried to control her words, to weave her pauses in naturally. But the truth was that she could barely bring herself to use a word that genuinely applied to Felipe, and to Karen's despicable, criminal, and almost-fiancé SS guard.

Karen nodded up a storm. "Oh God, Giselle. Great, great, great guys, but also drop-dead gorgeous. Jawline of a movie star, thick, curly hair. Maybe the straightest nose I've ever seen in my life. Like he was cut out of a magazine, you know?"

Every bit as casually as she sipped from a paper cup filled with lemonade, Karen said, "Good breeding, you know."

How could Giselle have such positive feelings toward Karen when she was capable of saying a thing like that without a second thought?

Good breeding.

But Giselle made herself nod. She had to get through this. Had to act enthralled, like a good friend, about some Aryan Nazi bastard.

"He sounds so handsome." Her voice didn't even sound like her own. "I don't suppose you have a picture of him?"

"No," Karen said sadly, momentarily sinking Giselle's heart. "Not on me, I mean. I do have one in an old shoebox under my bed at home. Maybe you should . . ."

Suggesting they get together without the girls seemed to be one of those things that brought out a shyness in Karen.

". . . come over for sangrias while Charlene stays with her parents and Elena has an evening with her dad?" Giselle asked.

"Yes!" Karen cried happily. "That sounds perfect."

"Agreed," said Giselle. "Perfect, perfect, perfect."

CHAPTER THREE

W hen he talked on the phone at home, especially when the conversation was an intense one, Daniel habitually paced back and forth as far as the rotini-curled cord would allow him to. It would have been easier to put the phone on speaker, but for him, that was primarily a function of the office phone; something about it felt so business-like that he hardly ever thought of using the speaker in his apartment.

Now, however, the gruff yet friendly voice of Colonel Judd poured through the living room, kitchen, and breakfast nook where Felipe sat with both his elbows on Daniel's desk, his hands clamped together in a prayer pose. Daniel, conscious of the missing weight of the receiver in his hand, went about his normal pacing. And Judd wasn't yet at the crux of the conversation.

Right now, he was explaining to them that he'd never imagined he would enjoy gardening, but now that he was retired, he could spend all weekend on his small but teeming patch of vegetables.

"Wife and I have gotten much healthier from it too," he said. "You know what grows like wildfire in Connecticut?"

Sensing that Daniel was on the verge of saying, "This isn't why we called, Judd," Felipe took a deep breath and said, "Glad you're enjoying retired life. Nice change of pace, I imagine."

"Everything you could want for salads," Judd answered himself. "Never gave a shit about a salad that didn't come alongside a steak as big as my head, but we can grow everything for ourselves now. We've got kale, we've got lettuce, cabbage, we got tomatoes . . ."

Fearing Judd was prepared next to list all the flora that Connecticut's topography allowed, Daniel said, "Sounds like a damn fine salad, Judd. But we need your *non*-gardening expertise for a minute here."

Felipe shook his head at Daniel.

Since leaving the army, Judd worked during the week as a consultant to an Israeli security company in New York— meaning that his version of "retired" was quite different from most people's. Most importantly, he still had access to the file containing all the interviews conducted on those left at the Paraguayan compound that he, Daniel, Felipe, and Giselle had raided years before.

Felipe explained the situation with Karen, starting with the inadvertent squiggle after her last name on the napkin and ending with Karen's suggestion that Giselle come over to get a look at Wolfgang's photograph.

"We should hear from Giselle anytime," Daniel added. "She's got a camera with her, and she's going to try to sneak a picture of this swine when Karen's out of the room. As long as all goes according to plan, she'll send that over asap—"

"And I'll check it against all the interview files," Judd supplied, the excitement in his voice even greater than when he'd bragged about homesteading meals. He readily agreed with Felipe's theory that Karen might be Hitler's niece by marriage, her mother Gretl being Eva Braun's sister.

"Glad we're all on the same page," Daniel said.

"Me too," Judd agreed.

"I'll have to get you boys out here for a meal sometime. Tell you, we get carrots like nobody's business. Got to be careful with the potatoes, these cold winters and all, but we still get some damn fine Russets. Wife's thinking about asparagus—"

"Judd, I hate to cut you short," Felipe said, "but Giselle should be calling any time, and I want to make sure we don't miss her. But homegrown baked potatoes and asparagus sound great. Let's make it happen sometime."

Daniel rolled his eyes as Felipe ended the call. "One of the toughest, most decorated soldiers ever to go after Hitler, and now all he cares about are goddamn Brussels sprouts."

"He never mentioned Brussels sprouts," Felipe said over his shoulder on his way to the kitchen to pour himself a drink.

"Maybe we should call him back and find out whether they grow this time of year in Connecticut."

"Think this is what I've got to look forward to when *I* retire?" Daniel called after him. "Telling people who call about lettuce?"

"I think what you've got to look forward to when *you* retire is flying pigs."

Daniel laughed. He was looking for the TV remote to see if a tennis match was on when the phone rang. Even though Felipe rushed back into the room with nothing more than ice in his glass, Daniel beat him to the receiver.

"Giselle?" he said in lieu of hello.

"Hello, uncle." The breathy eagerness in her voice was an auspicious sign. "Did you get a chance to talk to Judd?"

"Yes, and if we had a lack of knowledge about what goes in a salad, it's been dispelled."

"Um—"

"Never mind that."

He glanced up at Felipe, his eyes glistening with curiosity. "Were you able to get the picture?"

"No," she said right away. Then, not giving the men long enough to register their disappointment, she added, "I got something better."

~~~

It was possible that Karen was right about Wolfgang, that he was—objectively—a good-looking man, but Giselle couldn't get past her repulsion to judge. In sepia tones, the picture revealed a man with a broad nose, piercing eyes, and skin tattered by combat. It also revealed his uniform. Unfortunately, there was no telltale insignia, but the man had accoutrements that made Giselle's stomach churn. A helmet belted to his chin. A sash of long, sharp bullets draped over his neck. Karen was talking, but Giselle wasn't listening. She was trying to memorize a criminal's face, itching to take the picture that Judd could check against his files.

"I'm sorry." Giselle took a long sip of her Coca Cola. "What were you saying?"

"Distracted by how handsome he is, aren't you? I was just saying, I'm lucky Hans has zero interest in old picture albums." Karen ran a finger over the picture's edge. "I would hate to part with this one."

"Would Hans be jealous?" Giselle asked.

A pleasant, spacey look took hold of Karen.

"Nah." She tapped the picture. "Unlike *this* guy, Hans isn't the jealous type. He's a good guy." Giselle couldn't put her finger on what it was, but there was something different about how Karen was talking about Hans tonight. She'd spoken fondly of him on many occasions, but her tone tonight was the dreamy sort normally found in couples who've just started dating or just married, and Giselle felt sure Karen would've mentioned by now if she and Hans had eloped in the night.

"A *really* good guy," Karen said, closing the album on Wolfgang's menacing stare. Giselle watched where Karen placed the album, mentally bookmarking the approximate place in it where she could find Wolfgang's picture again as soon as Karen left the room.

"Hey, I'm really glad you came over," Karen said.

Maybe she just gets gushy when she's drinking, Giselle thought. That could account for how romantically she lingered on Hans's name tonight. Though Giselle wasn't even sure that Karen was drinking. At the start of the night, Giselle had declined the offer of wine, saying she had an early morning appointment—but truthfully, she just didn't want to lose any sharpness. She was there not only for the picture but, as always, for any clues Karen might drop as she became more comfortable in Giselle's presence.

In the spirit of accommodating her guest, Karen had saved them both Cokes. Giselle had assumed Karen switched to wine at some point for herself, but looking at her glass now, Giselle could see a few loitering bubbles of carbonation.

"It was nice of you to invite me," Giselle said.

She was going to have trouble making her tone match the warm looseness of Karen's. Every time Giselle was around her lately, she found herself thinking of actors in serious movies—how strange it would be to live a life where you were always pretending to think and feel things you didn't. Giselle was beginning to loathe it.

"No, I mean,"—Karen kicked off her shoes and drew her feet onto the couch—"it's good to have a girlfriend. I've got Hans, and I couldn't ask for a better boyfriend, but it's been a very long time since I had any female friends."

Giselle smiled. "It's hard to make friends when you're an adult," she said with some genuine sympathy. "When you're a kid, there's so much built-in playtime. When you're grown up . . ."

"You make friends with kids' parents."

"Exactly. *Sometimes.*"

"But still. I've been nannying for a while, but I guess it's not the same. The nanny doesn't make friends with the mothers that often. And even when I've met someone who seemed like a potential friend . . . I don't know." She looked at Giselle with sudden directness. "Do you ever find it hard to trust people?"

"All the time," Giselle answered automatically, before she could stop herself.

From the steadiness of her gaze, it appeared that Karen may dig into this comment, but Giselle reckoned she probably decided to leave it alone because asking Giselle to divulge her trust issues would've invited reciprocation. This felt like a prime opportunity, but Giselle couldn't figure out exactly how to proceed, or what to give up in order to elicit the right private detail from Karen.

She couldn't very well say, "*I don't trust people because the bank I worked for was colluding to pump money into Hitler's compound in Paraguay, where he was medically experimenting on children no older than my daughter. And I suspect he's your uncle.*"

She opened her mouth.

"Hey, no need," Karen said. "The way I see it, we all came from somewhere, right? And it's not always easy to talk about. If you've got stuff . . . I've got stuff too. Maybe that's why I feel like you get me."

"Maybe," Giselle said, her voice barely above a whisper.

Perhaps it was the quiet intimacy of the moment, but Giselle nearly jumped out of her skin when there was a knock at the door. To be fair, whoever it was knocked as though the building was on fire and he was there to warn them.

The light scowl playing on Karen's eyebrows disappeared as soon as she opened the door. "Nils!" she greeted the young man at the door. What immediately struck Giselle about him was that he seemed solid in every way—good posture, head held high, shoulders back—except for his eyes, which were skittish, darting left to right. His hair was a light, feathery blond usually seen on children. He couldn't have been older than twenty.

He spoke in a rush: "Hello, Karen, I hope you're not busy. I came by from studying because I needed to tell you—"

Then his nervous eyes stopped on Giselle.

"I didn't realize you had company." Looking at a spot between the women, possibly unsure who to direct his comment to, Nils said, "I apologize for interrupting. I'll come back later."

"Don't be ridiculous." Karen ushered him inside and closed the door. "Giselle, this is my cousin, Nils. He's studying economics at the University of Buenos Aires, and he's at the top of his class."

Nils blushed profoundly but nevertheless nodded in agreement with these facts about himself.

"And this is my good friend Giselle. She came over tonight so we could reminisce about boys." She bumped her hip into Nils, who seemed at a complete loss for how to respond to this playfulness.

"It's nice to meet you, Giselle, but I will let you two enjoy your evening. I'll come back when you're free."

"Nils, relax. Tell me what you came by for. You want something to drink?"

Ignoring the question, he replied, "I came by to discuss a . . . family matter. I wouldn't bore your friend with it. We can talk later." His voice was as insistent as he dared allow it to be.

Giselle felt she could read the young man fairly well: he couldn't talk about anything to do with family that involved Hitler around a stranger, but he also couldn't arouse suspicion in the stranger. He had to appear that he was withdrawing for reasons of pure politeness, and Karen was not making it easy for him.

"Fine," she said suddenly. "But I'm going to show you how much I trust Giselle—and you, for that matter." Karen rolled her eyes, presumably at her cousin's seriousness, but then her expression became . . . reflective. She breathed in deeply.

"I would like my dear friend and my dear cousin to be the first ones I tell. Other than Hans, of course."

The comment was a giveaway. Giselle understood before Karen spoke why she'd been happy to go along with soda over wine for the night, why she was moony when she talked of her betrothed. Giselle thought it just as Karen said it.

"I'm pregnant."

Instinctively, Karen's hands covered her abdomen like a shield. Her smile quaked in her effort not to cry.

Giselle wished she hadn't been so focused on Wolfgang earlier in the night. Had she been paying better attention to the signs with Karen, maybe she could have predicted this and felt less stymied now. She could have mentally prepared herself for how she could—how she *should*—react to a divulgence as unimaginably personal as this one. Karen stood there positively glowing. Nils, surprisingly, came out of his shell in response to the news. Hugging Giselle, smiling ear to ear, babbling about how she had always been a wonderful older cousin to him and what a wonderful mother she would make.

Meanwhile, Giselle just sat there. For a moment, she feared that while Karen was the one with an excuse to feel sick, she would be the one to throw up. A growing body of evidence suggested that this woman was her enemy. She had to simultaneously push down a feeling of true happiness for Karen's news, reminding herself who this was, and drum up a reaction that reflected that joy she was trying not to feel. It threatened to overwhelm her: feeling torn in every direction. Being considered a trustworthy friend by someone who called Hitler "uncle." Suddenly she could not wait to get home to Felipe and have him hold her.

"Giselle, you're so quiet," Karen said, with a note of hurt in her voice.

Swallowing the bile and shaking herself out of her trance, Giselle stood up. She crossed the room to hug Karen. "Please forgive me. I'm sitting there so out of it." Giselle pulled back and looked Karen in the eyes. "Of course I'm happy for you. If you're happy, I'm happy. And I know how much you've wanted a baby."

"I *am* happy, yes. I'm ecstatic."

Apparently in a more trusting mood in light of this news, Nils explained to Giselle, "Karen has wanted to be a mother since I was a baby. She was only, what, six or seven, but she would tell people I was her baby. Do you remember that, Karen?"

"I still tell people you're my baby." She nudged him playfully, and this time he laughed.

"Yes, of course, you're such a . . . 'baby person,'" Nils said.

Giselle babbled, "it's only . . . well, it's a surprise, I guess. I was thinking this news would come along sometime after the wedding."

"You and me both," Karen said. "It's definitely ahead of where we saw ourselves, but we talked about it, and we're both over the moon. It'll mean bumping up the wedding for sure . . . which I'd like to talk to you"—she looked at Giselle and put a warm hand on her shoulder—"about later. No matter where we are in the timeline, I just couldn't be happier."

"Tante Lotte will be shocked," Nils said.

As Karen was telling Nils that's exactly why they weren't going to be explicit about *why* the wedding was getting moved up—they were just going to be "in a hurry to start their lives together." Giselle found herself distracted at the mention of Karen's mother, *Tante Lotte*. Nils came here to discuss a family matter. Giselle was eager to get back on track with her investigation but knew she couldn't rush the moment.

"Hmm," Giselle said. "I don't suppose this 'family matter' you were here to discuss is a baby shower for Karen, then?"

Nils said, "No, I'm afraid not," in a relaxed-enough tone, looking at Karen as if he was waiting for approval.

"It is celebratory though. We'd . . ." He strung out the word in a last bit of hesitation, but Karen made no move to stop him from speaking.

"We'd like to throw a birthday party for your mother. A surprise party."

"Who's 'we'?" Karen asked, saying exactly what Giselle was thinking.

"A couple of her very close neighbors and myself. But since you are so festive—"

"You'd like me to host the party?"

"It would make Mother so happy."

Giselle's wheels immediately began to spin. She needed to get herself invited to this party. For the moment, she staved off the queasy knowledge that it would mean to be swarmed by Hitler's family—and thereby closest allies—all night. It was an *in*.

She was putting together the exact words to offer her assistance with the party when Karen said, "I'd be glad to host. Hell, I love throwing a party. But I'm already finding myself exhausted by the morning sickness. I don't suppose I could count on my best friend to help me out for the night?"

Giselle didn't know what to do with the words Karen had chosen to express herself. She couldn't think about it. She *wouldn't* think about it. She broadened her actor's smile.

"Of course you can count on me. I'd love to help out."

~~~

In his apartment, Daniel looked at Felipe, who had put the phone back on speaker to hear his wife's explanation of this turn of events. His ice cubes were melting with nothing to keep them cold.

"Giselle, this is wonderful news," Felipe cried. Not thinking, he swallowed the melted ice.

Daniel, for his part, stopped pacing the floor like a bull ready to charge a matador. Felipe thought, once again, that Daniel's angry face looked a great deal like his excited face. In this case, of course, his stern brow and tight facial muscles meant he was very excited about the opportunity presented to them. The fact that his heavy strides had stopped could only mean one thing: he had a plan.

"Excellent work, Giselle," he offered first. As fond as she ordinarily was of her uncle's praise, she now said nothing and waited for him to proceed.

"We must set you up to make a good impression on these people."

"What are you thinking?" Felipe asked.

Daniel leaned over the phone to make sure he was heard clearly. "I want you to offer to pay for several things at this event—flowers, champagne, that sort of thing. At my expense, of course."

"Won't it seem odd?" Giselle asked, sounding more timid than Daniel was accustomed to. Maybe it wasn't timidity; maybe she was simply tired. It had not gone overlooked that she was bearing most of the grunt work for this mission so far.

"You say this woman considers you a good friend—one of her best friends?"

"She does, yes."

"Then go with that. If she questions the purchases, say you are grateful for the friendship and that you insist on these contributions as a gesture. Emphasize that you're grateful to meet her family and stress that you want to make a good impression on them," Daniel explains.

"She'll take it as an indication that you plan on being a close friend of hers for years. Play this right and she'll come out trusting you more—not less."

Felipe wrinkled his brow. "And that's the point of buying the flowers and champagne? Make a gesture and solidify the friendship?" There was nothing explicitly wrong with the idea, but they'd been following this track since the beginning of Operation Karen, as he sometimes thought of it. He'd felt certain Daniel had something more up his sleeve.

Not one to disappoint, Daniel said, "Of course not. That's a side benefit. You offer these things, Giselle, because it will make it much less suspicious when you also offer to pay for a photographer at the event."

"Uncle Daniel, no," Giselle said automatically. "They'll never go for it. You should have seen Nils when he saw me in the apartment. This is not a group that's going to allow—"

"That's okay," said Felipe, following along with Daniel's thought process. "When they object—and they'll probably do so on the grounds that it would cost too much on top of everything else you're paying for—"

"That's when I offer to photograph the event myself," Giselle finished. She normally loved it when the three of them were so much on the same page that they seemed capable of reading each other's minds, but she was still mentally drained from the afternoon. And no matter how great an opportunity she knew it was, she could not yet bring herself to be excited about attending this party—let alone bankrolling it.

"Yes!" Daniel said. "They won't be able to say no without looking suspicious, and you'll have Karen vouching for you."

"Maybe Nils too, at this point," Felipe said.

"Maybe Nils too," Daniel repeated. "Offer to turn over all the film to them if they claim shyness or privacy or anything else. Obviously, you'll keep a roll of film for yourself, and we'll get Judd on working out these bastards' identities straight away."

It was a good plan. Giselle did her best to muster enthusiasm for it, which Felipe had no trouble doing. He couldn't stop pointing out that this was great news.

Giselle couldn't stop thinking about the piece of information she hadn't passed along to the rest of the team.

After Nils left, Karen and Giselle stood around the island in Karen's kitchen sketching out preliminary ideas for the party. They laughed several times as they attempted to incorporate what Karen named as her mother's main interests in life—eating Zurich ragout with white wine and sometimes leaving out the ragout. Somewhere along the way, Giselle had said, "You know, I really am happy for you," and she hadn't immediately known which part of her it came from: the part playing a role designed to dupe a target, or the part that had been, for some time, as lonely for a friend as Karen was.

Misunderstanding why Giselle was so pensive, Karen said, "Hey look. You certainly don't have to spell it out—we all need privacy about some things—but whatever's making your husband hesitate to have another baby, I really hope he'll change his mind soon."

"Thank you," Giselle said, thinking of exactly what it would take to get him to change his mind. "Stranger things have happened."

Putting away their party ideas for the time being, Karen said, "Tell me about it. Who knows—maybe we'll even be pregnant at the same time. Selfishly speaking, I would not mind having a friend to go through everything with."

Giselle couldn't help thinking that if she were pregnant, at least she would have an excuse for this nausea constantly threatening to spill out of her.

CHAPTER FOUR

With an expert flick of her wrist, Giselle applied another coat of mascara—much blacker than the evening sky outside Karen's bathroom window—to lashes that arched beautifully toward her thick, dark eyebrows. She wasn't what anyone in their right minds would have called vain, she was much more concerned with remaining fierce enough to be considered an honorary Mossad agent than rival Audrey Hepburn as the face of Maybelline—but this time, Giselle couldn't help herself from taking a long, appreciative assessment of her reflection.

What a shame Felipe can't be here, she thought. The sight of her dressed up and made-up always seemed capable of stirring him from a funk, at least momentarily.

But she hadn't slipped into the bathroom to fawn over her appearance or thicken the fringe around her dramatically dark eyes. Just like everything else Giselle would do that night, this brief departure from the party was strategic.

When she stepped out of the relative quiet of Karen's bathroom, she was struck by the festive energy humming through the apartment: a medley of sounds that didn't need to be loud to describe the scene of Lotte's fifty-second birthday. Nils's—far more excitable than he seemed when Giselle met the nervous boy days before—was regaling some of Karen's younger relatives with tales of university life. The twinkle of voices stuck to lighthearted, party-appropriate topics. Ice clinked against the sides of crystal flutes.

What Giselle didn't hear were whispered conversations laced with suspicion. Monitoring for this had been her true purpose in stepping away from the living area into the bathroom under the guise of "freshening up." If Lotte, Nils, or any of the partygoers had found it necessary to question Karen about this stranger in their midst, perhaps even to chastise her for letting anyone snap their photos who did not also share their superior blood, well, this was their chance. But the levels of banter and mild drunken laughter stayed steady.

Giselle rejoined them with a nonchalant smile and several of them reciprocated the gesture. It seemed that when Karen had vouched for Giselle earlier that evening—with an enthusiasm that momentarily tugged at Giselle's heart despite herself—the family didn't question her.

So, they take Karen's word very seriously, Giselle thought. *They all trust her.*

Giselle had contributed more than her photographic skills to the evening. Lavender and white orchids adorned the room, and champagne bubbled in glasses several times already refilled, all thanks to Giselle. Well, thanks to Daniel also, but of course no one had a clue about that. Giselle knew these efforts presented her as nothing more than the eager friend. It helped that Karen had sung praises for her generosity.

"Giselle! There you are." Karen beckoned her over. "I want you to meet someone." Giselle moved toward Karen with a cultivated grace. She was naturally sure-footed, but on top of that, she was aware that a shoulders-back, chin-high sort of poise was likely to go over well with this crowd.

Even as she moved, she held the camera at chest height, ready at a moment's notice to hoist it and trigger the mechanism that would commit to film even the most fleeting moment of this party.

Evidence.

Giselle turned the word over like a worry stone. She may be answering to her own name and without a disguise, but she was still undercover—and managing one of the most delicate balancing acts of her life.

Standing elbow to elbow with Karen and half listening to her introduction of a mutual acquaintance of her and Charlene's mother, Marcia, Giselle kept one eye on "Lotte," an elegant blonde woman despite the faint age lines etched around her eyes and mouth. Giselle heard it was Gretl Braun's beauty that captivated the monster she married, and as much as she hated to admit it, she could understand.

At fifty-two, the woman still had expertly-pruned eyebrows that arched over her dark, shining eyes and faded mid-temple.

Her short curls betrayed no effort; they fell loose but were smooth around her ears.

Her mouth was lush and berry-red, though it cocked up menacingly on one side, in the same way one of her eyebrows frequently climbed higher than the other. It made her appear smug. A strong, confident woman, seemingly above everything going on around her. Someone who'd grown accustomed to reaping all the deference, fanfare, and pampering that came with being a royal.

Or so Giselle imagined. She couldn't help it: part of her still hoped she was wrong. That they were all wrong.

"Such a charming little gathering, nicht wahr?" Lotte remarked, her voice a well-modulated melody. "It reminds me of. . ." she paused, a wistful smile playing upon her lips. "Well, of simpler times, shall we say?"

Simpler times indeed, Giselle thought.

She forced a smile as she snapped a picture of Karen and her acquaintance, arms linked, foreheads tilted toward each other. Giselle wanted to make sure she distributed her attention in a way that didn't arouse suspicion.

Lowering the camera now and swiveling to Lotte with the same breezy smile still plastered on her face, Giselle offered a simple laugh and said, "I can't say that I've ever known Buenos Aires to be a simple place. I assume your hometown was rural in comparison to all this bustle?"

That's it, she encouraged herself. *Make them think you have no idea what this family's history could be—while pumping them for any information that will help us seal their fate.*

"I wouldn't call it rural, not quite." Lotte paused, pursing her bow-shaped mouth as she seemed to contemplate Giselle's face. Her eyes flicked almost imperceptibly to Karen. It wasn't the first, nor would it be the last, time a member of Karen's innermost circle appeared to check in with her for subtle verification that it was okay to share what they were about to. Karen's unspoken reply was always the same: she offered a loose, comfortable smile and ever so slightly inclined her forehead. A positive response as enthusiastic as she dared.

"No," Lotte continued, "it had a chaotic sort of charm, but nothing to compare with the vibrant energy of this city."

Giselle shrugged innocently. "I've been here so long, I guess I take the feel of things here for granted. To the point that I don't even see them?" She added an inflection of question to this—patently false—statement to engage Lotte. And it worked.

With a one-sided smile, Lotte rolled her eyes good-naturedly at Giselle, the way Giselle could imagine doing in response to Karen or Nils. Right away Giselle laughed lightly, determined to connect with this woman however she could.

"That happens," Lotte allowed. "Though typically with more with someone who is, say, fifty-two years old. Perhaps even older. You're far too young to say you've lived anywhere long enough to take it for granted."

"You may be right."

Karen eagerly tugged over a white rail-back chair for Giselle and then one for herself. "Sit, sit!" she urged, obviously thrilled to watch her dearest friend in Buenos Aires getting on famously with her mother—who, just then, was tsk-tsking Karen.

"You're always doing that. Dragging chairs across your beautiful wooden floor. You're going to—"

"—scuff it beyond repair," Karen joined in, apparently having memorized the chastisement for all its repetitions.

"So, what is 'chaotic charm,' exactly?" Giselle asked, still smiling.

"Oh, there was so much happening there when I was a girl, so much upheaval." Lotte briefly made eye contact with her seatmate on the couch, a woman who appeared to be around her own age but with a permed mop of rust-colored hair and small glasses that gave her whole face a pinched look. Whoever this was sighed lightly and then stood up under the guise of needing to stretch her legs.

Wasn't there a third Braun sister?

It was clear to Giselle the woman was uncomfortable with the direction in which this conversation threatened to veer.

She averted her eyes from Giselle as she meandered over to the dessert table, which was topped with exquisitely layered Choco Orta, vanilla alfajores ringed with coconut shavings, and a Rogel cake. The whole thing made for a relatively undifferentiated, earthy color palette—which unnerved the party planner within Giselle (her wedding with Felipe had been explosively colorful). But Karen had raved about these flavors. In fact, when she'd shared her mother's predilection for dulce de leche, Giselle had been the one to suggest the Rogel.

Now she simultaneously lifted the heavy camera to her eye, focused in on the red-haired woman under the guise of photographing the confectionary spread, and asked Lotte, now out of her range of vision, "May I be so bold as to ask what you think of the Rogel cake?"

She snapped the photo just as Lotte let loose a hearty laugh.

"A little bird told me you were the one responsible for the Rogel cake. I believe you came here prepared to impress." Giselle turned back in time to catch Lotte's pouty-lipped smile. "And you did, my dear."

Karen squeezed Giselle's arm and briefly laid her head on her shoulder, pleased by her mother's embrace of her new companion. For Giselle, the thought segued into an image of Karen introducing Lotte to Hans. What must have Lotte thought of *him*?

Giselle's eyes skimmed the room for him as nonchalantly as possible. She had finally met him earlier that evening, and her impression of him had been . . . mixed to say the least. It was more accurate to say that he was photogenic than to say he was a handsome man. Hair that had cut a dramatic silhouette in black and white appeared mouse-brown in person, with bangs his eyes seemed content to hide behind. Giselle instantly picked up that his preferred way to stand was with his back leaning against something—the counter, the wall, the refrigerator—with his hands clasped behind him, and his body leaning forward, shoulders hunched toward the ground.

She imagined him now in the kitchen, huddled in a corner, anxiously wetting his lips between tiny sips of lager. Clearly, Giselle had concerns pressing enough to render Karen's choice of mate meaningless, but she couldn't help lingering on the thought of why a bubbly, outgoing, social, dynamic woman like Karen would choose someone who could barely lift his eyes from the (amazingly unscuffed) floorboards?

Maybe, Giselle thought, *Karen just attracts cowards.* She didn't care if her conclusion wasn't fair. She thought of Wolfgang's smug face, safe under protective equipment his successor would never have. *Maybe these are the men who glom onto women like Karen and Lotte—sniveling, gutless monsters.*

She breathed. In through her nose: two, three, four. Hold it for a second. Out through her almost imperceptibly parted lips: two, three, four, five, six. Felipe had learned this calming breathing technique in combat, and she used it now to keep her anger from roaring out of control. She also needed to keep in mind that Karen and Lotte themselves, no matter how charming under indoor party lights, were no small part of the problem she was here to annihilate.

With a sigh, she said to Lotte, "I suppose we have our share of upheaval here, too. I'll remember forever when Plaza de Mayo was bombed."

She allowed herself to visibly shudder. It was true that the Argentinian Navy and Air Force's strike stuck with her as though it had occurred months ago rather than nearly ten years ago, but still, she was going somewhere with this.

She was going somewhere with all of it.

"Did you already live here then?" Giselle asked.

"That happened in the summer, didn't it?" Lotte helped without actually answering.

"I hope the upheaval you mentioned in your own hometown was nothing like that." Inhale—two, three. "Did you say where that was?"

Maybe she had asked it just casually enough. Maybe the woman simply felt there was no getting out of saying it. By any account, she looked at Giselle and, without so much as a slowed-down blink, said, "Munich, dear."

"I didn't tell you that?" Karen asked, the faintest hint of nervousness in her voice.

Giselle shrugged; she knew how to appear perfectly casual, even when she felt her heart trying to chew its way out of her chest.

"Possibly."

Issuing a lighthearted laugh at herself, she said, "Geography has never been my strong suit. I have to admit that counts for names of countries and cities too—to me, Germany is just Germany."

She had decided instantaneously on the tactic of playing, if not dumb, the part of a young woman. One who'd led a privileged life, untouched by detailed knowledge of which parts of Germany had spawned which Hitler loyalists, and which had served—proudly—as Nazi strongholds.

Giselle decided she would further flaunt her ignorance. "What sort of upheaval did you have there? If you don't mind," she rushed to add. "I hope nothing unpleasant. This is a party, after all." She let her fake self-conscious smile sell her innocence.

"A very nice one," a third voice chimed in.

Giselle looked up in the direction of the voice and upon seeing Nils, her heart dropped. He plopped into the seat abandoned by the red-haired woman, next to Lotte. Giving her a brief affectionate squeeze on the shoulders, he said, "Hello, Tante. How are you enjoying your beautiful party?"

"Perhaps not as much as you are." She gave him an uneven smile, from which Giselle could easily unpack the playful ribbing from aunt to nephew about his drinking. Despite the fact that she'd met him for only the second time in her life tonight, even Giselle could see the marked difference in the way he carried himself after a few beers. Everything about him, from his stiff joints to his staccato manner of speaking—had loosened.

So young, Giselle thought, *but so dangerous.*

Part of Giselle wanted to leap for joy when Lotte was the one to steer them back to the conversational track they'd been on, not taking Nils's arrival for the natural distraction it could have been.

"I was just telling Karen's lovely friend what it was like growing up in Munich."

Part of Giselle seized up in worry. The wording felt pointed, daring almost. As though Lotte were making the odd choice to show her timid nephew how expertly she could navigate a discussion with a stranger—one about a girlhood that coincided with Hitler closing his fist around the pride of Bavaria.

It would appear Nils had as little idea what to make of this as Giselle did. She watched him try for eye contact with Karen, who in turn sought her mother's eyes, which were locked without menace or anxiety on Giselle.

"Oh, nothing that tragic, not that touched my world."

Giselle locked her features in place. Pretended she was the Mona Lisa—painted still and unreadable.

On the inside, she processed Gretl Braun boasting of a life untouched by tragedy.

"When I was a little thing, the Poland consulate opened in our city. That was something I remember my mother and father having strong opinions about."

As opposed to the long-lashed, doe-eyed image she'd painted of herself tonight, Giselle had become somewhat of a history buff over the foregone years. Calls it her own preoccupation. While her husband beat the bushes for any sign of Hitler and otherwise numbed himself from the pain of living, she left off caring for Elena mostly to pick up books that placed unspeakable horrors in some context.

Especially after having Elena, she didn't plan to be on the frontlines of battle again, not in the way Felipe and even Uncle Daniel did. Not because she couldn't, but because she wouldn't. She was Elena's shield in this world, and she wouldn't leave Elena unprotected to the devil himself—aka, Adolf Hitler.

So, she read.

She had set down nighttime books containing fables where animals of every species learned how to get along and respect one another, and to the sound of her little girl sleeping in the next room, had thumbed through every book and newspaper article on the nightmares she could find.

In that moment, Giselle remembered reading about an event that occurred in 1920, when dear old Tante Lotte remembered her parents "having opinions" on the opening of the Polish consulate. That year, the Nazi paramilitary Sturmabteilung and the Nazi newspaper *Völkischer Beobachter* established their headquarters in Munich.

"Oh, and several wonderful museums opened when I was a girl," Lotte said, her eyes drifting away to some fond memory. "I'll always remember because my mother was such a fan of them."

"Was she," Giselle answered without the inflection of a question. She felt that her words were too clipped, her tone too icy for a stranger's divulgence of her late mother's beloved pastime, but it was better than screaming at the woman—better than throttling her.

"I didn't know that," Nils said, his eyes undecided on where to land.

Karen, in a voice detectably low given her normally robust timbre, said, "Yes, Grandmother was a fan of art." If Giselle wasn't mistaken, there was an iciness to Karen's voice as well—toward her mother.

She doesn't like whatever game her mother's playing.

"Yes. Take the Lenbachhaus museum. What a beautiful affair it was. Have you seen it?" Lotte asked Giselle without even pretending to want an answer. "This grand, palatial villa. After the Florentine style. It ended up housing some world-class Munich masters."

Munich masters.

If Giselle wasn't mistaken, the Lenbachhaus had opened its doors in 1929, the year before another "Munich master" had given his campaign speech in preparation for the German federal election. Two years before Brown House became home to the National Socialist Party. Three years before Munich opened its gates, its arms, its heart to the Sicherheitsdienst—the Nazi intelligence agency.

Inhale for two, three, four.

Exhale for two, three, four, five, six . . .

~~~

"Why does it work?" Giselle had whispered to Felipe the first time she'd heard him talk about this method of breathing. They had been in bed, Elena nestled between them. Felipe had just instructed the little girl how to "calm breathe" to help her settle down after the nightmare that had brought her barreling into their bedroom.

"When you breathe in," Felipe said, "it activates the part of the nervous system that prepares for situations of survival."

"Fight or flight?" She remembered they had been smiling at each other as though the topic of conversation had been much more flirtatious than it actually was.

"Exactly. But when you exhale, it activates a different part of the nervous system. One that's associated with the passing threat. So, when you make yourself exhale for a long time on purpose, it's a way of telling your brain and your body that—"

"Everything's okay again?" Giselle had supplied.

She remembered him nodding before turning on his back and looking up at the ceiling.

~~~

Before Lotte could go on telling Giselle about the grand openings of any more art museums, Giselle said, "You have a different idea of 'upheaval' than I." She laughed, perhaps too loudly, in an effort to offset any hostility implied by the words themselves.

Sitting at Giselle's left, Karen cleared her throat, which Giselle took as her cue to lob a softball question Lotte's way.

"Did your mother's love of art stay with you?"

Nils was absentmindedly picking at the paper wrapper on a cupcake and transferring flecks of icing onto his thumb in the process. He was getting nervous. The lubrication supplied by his drink was wearing off, and without another good oiling soon, he was likely to grow overly suspicious of Giselle—no matter how much interference Karen ran.

And was it just Giselle's imagination, or was Karen herself acting on edge about this entire interaction? Fortunately, Giselle didn't feel it was aimed at her. Karen only seemed uncomfortable with her mother's behavior, but she was uncomfortable, nonetheless. If Lotte noticed her daughter or nephew's antsiness or misgivings, she did not let on.

"Why yes,"

Turning to Karen with a certain sharpness—transformed, perhaps, by her own recollection of the past into the harder-edged, more ambitious creature she had been prior to retiring in Buenos Aires—Lotte said, "Tochter, do you remember me telling you about my photography days?"

Karen rolled her eyes playfully and let them land on Giselle.

"Oh, *once or twice*," she over-enunciated, betokening the countless times Lotte must have regaled her with stories of these so-called "photography days."

Sipping from her glass, which sparkled under the cool violet-white lighting of Karen's den, Lotte nodded meaningfully toward Giselle and said, "I'll have you know I attended the Bavarian State School of Photography. I was quite something."

"That's impressive," Giselle said under her breath. And she did indeed sound impressed—but intrigued is more accurately how she felt.

Gretl Braun—a photographer?

This wasn't a detail she'd come across, but there wasn't a great deal known about The Other Braun Sister.

"It sounds like such a prestigious institution. When did you attend?"

Rather than answer—*did she fear the date would have somehow been a giveaway?*—Lotte said, "I photographed well before then, though. The school was where I honed my craft, but I had a natural flair for it that earned me some level of recognition even before then."

Giselle allowed her mouth to fall gently agape as she lowered the camera demurely to her lap.

"Suddenly I feel inadequate." She smiled.

"She's very good," Nils said, his voice somewhat returned to the straightlaced timbre that hinted at how tightly wound he was. He didn't even bother elucidating who he was testifying to and whom about.

Giselle brought the camera back to eye level.

"Please do not, my dear," Lotte said with a smile more drawn than her previous.

"I would never take pictures at my own party. I'm afraid I'm far too vain. I'd be taking pictures of myself in the mirror all night!"

Giselle politely laughed and Karen said, "Don't encourage her—it's true," and Nils let his eyes linger on Giselle's camera.

"What was your involvement in photography before the school?" Giselle asked.

"I worked for a rather prominent photographer." Lotte turned her still-glazed eyes toward Karen. "I believe I told you about him, dear."

"The one you and—" Nils cut himself off too obviously. His truncated sentence sat there like an unloaded pistol. Not technically a threat to the family's cover, but it made the tone suddenly dangerous.

It was a thing unsaid about the past.

But what?

With a staggered inhalation that briefly made Giselle think of passing along the breathing trick, Karen came to Nils's rescue. She wasn't thinking. She was automatically shifting into the mode of a gracious woman hurrying to save a social interaction on the verge of collapse.

"Your photography boss, yes. You mentioned him. He was the one who got you the apartment?"

The moment Karen said it, Lotte's eyes shot at her like daggers.

It was all Giselle could do to keep from gasping.

Her thought was only a theory—one she would need to bring to Uncle Daniel and Felipe right away so the three of them could madly sift for answers. She'd had a thought that neatly tethered the "Lotte" before her to Nazi Gretl, who was at the pinnacle of the hierarchy.

Suddenly she couldn't wait to get out of this room, out of this apartment, and away from these people. Now, it wasn't only about what it had been all night: the awareness. It kept hitting her in waves—she was elbow-to-elbow and effectively alone—in a room with someone who had not only cosigned the genocide of her people but enjoyed the notoriety that came with running in Hitler's illustrious circle. The thought of Daniel and Felipe considering Karen's innocence, seemed impossible.

Giselle felt it was time to take her own innocent act to a whole new level and throw in a note of humor sure to help set Lotte at ease again.

"An apartment you say? Was it all about your photography skills or was the boss maybe a little . . . wooed, shall we say?"

This ploy worked better than Giselle could've hoped: Lotte threw her head back to let loose a throaty laugh, one that even Hans peeked his head into the room like a prairie dog manifesting from its burrow.

"Well, Karen is mistaken, my dear. It wasn't my boss who obtained the apartment for us. More like the boss's boss. And he was certainly . . . charmed, if you will—not by my sister," Lotte said—with, if Giselle wasn't mistaken, a very slight slur. As if offering clarification on that very point, Lotte lifted her champagne flute to her self-satisfied lips and moderately gulped.

This was an unexpected ace up Giselle's sleeve, one that she had surprisingly not considered before. Lotte was relaxed enough to have become, as she would say in her native language *betrunken*. Now that Giselle thought about it, the woman had been nursing her champagne throughout their unnerving conversation; it was just that she seemed to be one of these people who didn't show symptoms until she made it unmistakably obvious.

Nils, on the other hand, showed every sign of having sobered up, the way a man would look upon having his face plunged in a bucket of ice water. He clearly didn't know what to say or do—but his features shifted, registering a grave response to something that had been said. And Giselle had an inkling, she knew exactly what.

~~~

After her relatives exchanged effusive goodbyes—even though they were all going to meet up at Lotte's favorite restaurant spot for salsa dancing—Karen slipped into the bathroom to freshen up for the remainder of the night. Giselle's deep sigh was timed perfectly with the clicking shut of the bathroom door. Then it was time to get to work.

Darting around the apartment without a clear idea of what she was looking for, Giselle spotted her first piece of take-home evidence on Karen's living room table. On the mahogany surface was a stack of mail so thick and disheveled Giselle was certain Karen merely grabbed it from the box and deposited it here without carefully examining its contents. She wouldn't miss a few pieces.

Stuffing these in the oversized, silky black bag she had chosen for this very purpose, Giselle continued to scan the contents with a seasoned detective's eye. She could hear sink water running in the bathroom, and Karen raised her voice to say, "Giselle, you better not be cleaning out there! Hans will help me with cleanup when we're back later."

Her line of sight flicked back and forth between the room and the bathroom door. Giselle called back, "If you insist. You two have some work to do though! Everyone appears to have had a very good time."

Saying it gave her an idea. She heard the faucet handle squeak close, and the whooshing water stopped as Giselle grabbed the crystal flute Lotte had been drinking from all night. Even in a rush, she understood the necessity of being careful. She used a napkin to grasp the glass from its base. She cradled it as carefully as possible among a handful of other napkins. She was tucking the flute into its nest when the door opened and Karen suddenly stood there, her natural beauty enhanced with nighttime makeup.

"Oh, believe me, he has some work to do tonight. You and I handled the preparation—Hans can step in for cleanup," she said.

~~~

After a short walk, they joined the rest of the group at a festively decorated table. Giselle managed to paste a veneer of normalcy on her face for the remainder of the evening, engaging in conversations about the weather and the latest cinema releases. Beneath the surface, her thoughts were churning, and her stomach was a tight knot of apprehension.

Karen's hand rested gently on her stomach, a subtle, but constant reminder of what was to come. An innocent child about to be born into this tangled web of secrets and danger. Giselle had to admit—despite her disgust at the family's potential history—Karen seemed . . . kind. Attentive. Maternal in a way that stirred a strange sense of longing within Giselle herself. How desperately she wished Felipe could see that the darkness could lift—that a better world was possible.

CHAPTER FIVE

The sterile efficiency of Swiss bureaucracy did little to soothe Felipe's mounting frustration. He sat back in Daniel's stiff office chair, folding the piece of paper on which he'd taken notes after speaking to the administrator at the University of Buenos Aires.

Unfolded it. Folded it back onto itself again, as he'd been doing for longer than he cared to think about.

Daniel's apartment in Geneva had become a makeshift war room. Maps of Buenos Aires adorned the walls, annotated with Felipe's notes hastily jotted in bright red marker. On the whiteboard, chaotic bursts of names, dates, and potential connections bloomed—arrows and question marks linking one tangle of words to the next.

Nils Hoffman. The name had become both an enigma and a nagging accusation. Felipe had spent hours poring over university records, the mundane details of an apparently above-average student's transcript suddenly representing a portal into the past. Or, at least, this had been Felipe's fervent hope.

In reality, his efforts had yielded the barest of facts:

A birth date, just over twenty years ago

A local address

The boy excelled in mathematics, especially geometry—and in biological science, though he earned slightly lower marks in literature and history

He took architecture as an elective subject, in which he earned his highest grade.

Just what the world needs, Felipe had thought upon discovery of this little detail. *A young relative of Hitler's with a vision for building new structures.*

The address in particular was no trivial detail. Knowing where Nils lived *had* to shed some light on the peculiar living arrangements: the boy lived in an apartment complex with, apparently, Lotte and several of her closest companions—while Karen maintained her own place. In a sense, her own world.

What these unearthed facts did not provide, however, was a clue as to who Nils Hoffman actually was.

Felipe knew the drill well enough. Those who had fled after the Third Reich's collapse often shed their identities like a snake in its skin. The namenserklärung, the official legal declaration of a name change, was a key tool in tracing those elusive figures. Yet, no such document existed for anyone named Nils Hoffman. Searches for birth records across Germany and Austria meticulously narrowed down to the boy's birth year, yielded nothing. It was as if he had materialized out of thin air.

"Nils Hoffman." He repeated the name aloud, the words tasting like ash on his tongue. The boy had been introduced to Giselle with such casual certainty, yet everything about his existence screamed fabrication. Nils was no careless oversight; he was a deliberate deception.

But why?

Hitler was famously childless. Rumors of impotence whispered down through the years, tales of a man twisted by ideology, incapable of siring offspring. This left only a few possibilities, none of them reassuring. If Nils was truly related to the Hitler-Braun lineage, he had to be a descendant of one of the siblings. But those records were readily available, their stories well-documented. None had produced a male child during the time in question.

A sickening sense of doubt began to gnaw at Felipe. The chase—with its research that kept his mind and hands busy, and with its thrilling breakthroughs—had become a lifeline, a way to channel his grief and rage into something resembling purpose. Had he clung to the connection to Karen, mistaking her kindness for complicity simply because it offered a path forward? Had his need for retribution blinded him to the simple truth that she might be exactly who she appeared? A cheerful young woman who, coincidentally, shares a past similar to the Karen Fegelein who haunted his overworked imagination.

Waves of guilt washed over him, mingling with an exhaustion that went bone-deep. He brought to mind the hopeful smile Giselle had worn when he'd left for Geneva, promising quick, meaningful progress on a hunt that it seemed all their lives now revolved around. His calls back home carried carefully constructed excuses: loose ends to tie up, leads to follow that were best handled from Europe. In the quiet apartment that echoed with her absence, her trust felt like an unbearable weight.

The whiteboard stared back at him. He could chart the movements of Hitler's cronies, trace funds, and analyze escape routes. But when it came to the true danger, an ideology whose poison was constantly threatening to seep into the groundwater, he seemed to be flailing in the dark.

With a frustrated sigh, he slumped down in Daniel's armchair, the weight of his own helplessness heavy upon him. Perhaps he had been searching for something that could never be found. The Nazis, in their final death throes, had been meticulous in covering their tracks, erasing names and forging new identities. Nils could be anyone, the descendant of a faceless henchman or a carefully groomed successor to a legacy of hate and violence.

The truth was, Felipe was no longer sure what breakthrough he longed for. Unearthing a hidden Nazi heir wouldn't bring back the dead or erase the horrors etched into the very fabric of their lives. His quest for a neat, conclusive ending suddenly felt naive. The tendrils of evil had burrowed deep. They were in a battle against an idea, one that transcended individuals, and mere names on birth certificates offered little solace.

He had to return to Buenos Aires, to Giselle and Elena. His place was beside them, protecting what mattered, not chasing ghosts halfway across the world. But what would he even say? That all his carefully laid out plans had dissolved into thin air? That the monsters he hunted might simply be shadows, remnants of a past best left buried?

~~~

A strange emptiness settled over Giselle as she hailed a cab home from Lotte's prized salsa dancing spot, the echoes of forced laughter and stilted conversation still ringing in her ears. Her walk from the taxi to her own apartment building and up its interior staircase felt mechanical. The click of her party heels on the sidewalk and then on the metal steps acted as a sleep-making metronome.

And tired is exactly what Giselle felt—overwhelmingly so. The uptick in energy she'd experienced, sparked by the vague impression that information about Lotte and her "photography boss" was significant, had faded over the course of the night. Giselle's energy drained as she watched potential relatives of Hitler dance, protected the evidence she'd spirited away in her purse, pretended to drink more than she did, whispered to Karen on the sidelines—about pregnancy, men, and how exhausting yet fulfilling a family could be.

It had been all forced smiles and small talk, a strange charade of normalcy played out against the backdrop of her growing unease. She couldn't shake the feeling that a hidden play was being staged around her, its true purpose concealed behind a veil of pleasantries.

Each step toward her apartment door echoed hollowly in the dimly lit hallway.

A flicker of guilt registered when she came to a stop outside Mrs. Gonzalez's door. Felipe would've balked at the idea of leaving Elena with someone even as kind and trustworthy as the neighbor they'd known the longest—a grandmother of three with a cotton-candy perm.

Mrs. Gonzalez's warm smile greeted Giselle as she opened the door. Elena shuffled behind, approaching sleepily.

"Ah, there she is, my little princess," Mrs. Gonzalez cooed, scooping Elena into a hug. "We had a grand time, didn't we? Someone made a new friend tonight, too!"

Illustrating this point, Elena raised her hand just long enough for her mother to spot the small, purple stuffed animal she held.

Giselle smiled at Mrs. Gonzalez.

"You got this for her?"

"I couldn't resist. She told me she loved puppies, and I saw this one at the market yesterday and thought of her."

Tilting her head gently to look Elena in the eye under her heavily drooping lids, Giselle asked, "Does your dog have a name?"

Barely audible through her yawn, Elena said, "Dan. After Uncle . . ."

And just like that, midway through naming her favorite uncle—quite possibly one of her favorite people overall—Elena was off to sleep. She didn't even stir when transferred from one set of loving arms to the other.

"Thank you again, Mrs. Gonzalez," Giselle said, unable to keep the weariness from her voice. It had been years since they moved to this building and first met the woman who'd become Giselle's closest confidante outside of her husband and uncle. With a pang of sadness, she realized that in all that time, Mrs. Gonzalez—with her gentle fussing and endless supply of homemade cookies—was the closest person they had to family nearby.

"And your handsome husband," Mrs. Gonzalez asked, her eyes filled with genuine concern. "He'll be back from his travels soon, yes?"

Giselle forced a smile. "Oh, I imagine it won't be long now. Any day, really," she replied, hoping the brightness in her voice masked her uncertainty.

As she finally entered and closed the door to her own empty apartment, a wave of loneliness washed over her. The isolation of their situation and the endless waiting and worrying was starting to feel unbearable. Without Felipe's steady presence, without the shared burden of their secrets, their home had become a fragile echo chamber of what-ifs and worst-case scenarios.

As Giselle tucked Elena into bed, the emptiness of their apartment hit her with unexpected force. Felipe's absence loomed in every shadowed corner—his habitual half-finished coffee cup absent from the kitchen table. The scent of his sandalwood cologne, a comforting presence, had faded under the smells of spray cleaner, dishwashing soap, laundry, and Giselle's perfume.

Her hand hovered over the landline receiver, but a hesitation she couldn't immediately characterize held her back. She thought of what she *wanted* them to know—that her suspicions, deepening with every seemingly benign anecdote—still clashed with a part of her that wasn't alarmed at all. That a casual touch from the woman they suspected was Gretl Braun had repulsed her in a way no shower or sleep could wash away. She had to separate her feelings from what they *needed* to know for the case.

That she'd pilfered potentially incriminating mail from her "best friend's" home.

That she had in her possession a glass drank heavily from by Eva Braun's sister.

That Gretl—or "Lotte"—had a history as a photographer so prized that her "boss's boss" had fixed her up with an apartment.

As Elena settled into her own bed without fully waking, an idea came to Giselle. Not a fully formed plan—more an impulse born of desperation and a longing for the comfort of her small family reunited. She gently scooped her daughter up, the warmth of her sleeping body a lifeline in the quiet room.

"Mija," she whispered, pressing a kiss to Elena's soft hair. "We're going on an adventure."

They packed in a whirlwind. Clothes were tossed haphazardly into a suitcase, favorite stuffed animals carefully arranged on top. Elena, roused from her sleepy haze, bounced around excitedly, gleefully declaring "Daddy!" and "Uncle Daniel!" with no further context. There was a rustle of tissue paper as it was packed around delicate evidence. The rhythmic click of the suitcase lock. Elena's innocent joy was a stark contrast to the knot of determined tension in Giselle's stomach.

The night air was cool against her skin as she hailed a taxi, and Elena chattered beside her about introducing Uncle Daniel to the stuffed Dan and telling Daddy how he'd missed the lemon pie they baked yesterday and how she wished she could've packed him a slice of it because it was his favorite.

On the red-eye flight, sleep was elusive. Images of Lotte's carefully manicured hands and Karen's eager smile flickered in her mind. She watched Elena sleep peacefully, nestled against her side, and longed for the simplicity of childhood obliviousness.

With a surge of both trepidation and resolve, she made her decision. They would confront Felipe with the undeniable reality of their lives, a reality far removed from the theoretical horrors of the past. Perhaps seeing her, seeing Elena, would shatter whatever inertia kept him locked away in Geneva. It was a long shot, she knew, a gamble with stakes that terrified her. But she had to try.

Dawn painted the sky in soft hues of pink and orange as they finally landed in Geneva. The airport, bustling with morning energy, felt alien after the subdued hush of the plane. With a sleeping Elena in her arms, Giselle hailed another taxi. Only once seated as comfortably as possible in the taxi's worn, navy blue backseat did it occur to Giselle she hadn't taken time to change out of her party clothes. Granted, she had kicked her high heels off the moment she'd arrived home in favor of reasonable loafers that hugged her tired feet. However, she'd hardly given a second thought to her going-out dress and her makeup intended to fit right in at a dim, sultry salsa club.

The familiar address slipped off her tongue.

Daniel. Not only would he accept an unannounced change in plans, he may not even be particularly surprised to see her show up on his stoop. After all, this couldn't shock him nearly as much as when she'd shown up unbidden all those years ago.

Still, when they finally arrived and stood squarely in front of Daniel's door, Giselle hesitated. Elena stirred in her arms, murmuring, "Uncle Daniel" from the depths of a half-dream. Giselle's deep breath reverberated through her chest. Her knock reverberated through a still dew-sprinkled morning. This was it. It was time.

CHAPTER SIX

The door creaked open. Elena blinked sleepily at her great-uncle, who answered the door with his accustomed morning crankiness, already scowling and poised to berate whoever had thought it wise to disturb him before he was out of his robe.

Then he took in the sight before him. The hostile lines in his face melted to nothingness.

Behind him, Daniel's warm kitchen beckoned. The normalcy of it all, the sink full of dishes, the notes scribbled by the fridge, the faint hum of the coffee maker—felt like a blow somehow. Felipe had this, at least. A life still firmly planted in the present in some way. And she was happy for him. But she also couldn't help but think of the homey scene before her and the home she had just left.

This kitchen, not theirs.

This living room sofa to pace circles around, not theirs.

Here—not home.

Felipe, having been pacing, froze at the sight of them. Giselle placed a hand on Elena's back, and with a deep breath, stepped inside.

~~~

Elena's delighted squeals filled the living room as she danced around, her new stuffed dog clutched tightly in her hand. Though it wasn't discussed, the normalcy of Elena's playfulness touched each of the adults' weary souls like silk.

Felipe and Daniel sat across from each other at the kitchen table, the remnants of a hasty breakfast scattered between them. Felipe's eyes, usually so sharp and focused, held a flicker of vulnerability that tugged at Giselle's heart. If she were being honest, his initial appearance startled her. While she'd missed him terribly, in the grand scheme of things, she had seen her husband very recently; yet he looked like he'd aged five years. She could extrapolate worry from the deep lines in his forehead, a lack of sunshine in his sallow complexion, and sleeplessness in the faint bluish-purple smears under his watery eyes.

Giselle spread out her evidence: a bank statement, a crumpled piece of innocuous mail, and—most damningly—the empty flute, carefully packaged. The last item Daniel examined it in silence, then gestured for Felipe to take a closer look.

"I swiped these from Karen's apartment," Giselle said in a voice reduced to a rasp by the traversing of time zones and climates. "I think the glass is Lotte's. Well, Gretl's. But I can't be sure."

"This is great, Giselle!"

Giselle was, frankly, thrown by Daniel's booming support. While she had independently assessed the glass was worth something and the mail—at least part of it—promised to be valuable as well, by the time she'd arrived, she had nearly convinced herself they couldn't add up to anything more than the incomplete hints they had accumulated so far.

She was equally surprised to feel the tears playing at the corners of her eyes. Sometimes people don't notice how much they need someone else—someone close—to see and validate their struggles until it happens out of the blue and they are left speechless, as Giselle was then. It made the hours inside the stuffy plane fade. For Giselle, it felt so similar to coming home after being gone too long.

Encouraged to return the tenderness she suddenly felt nourished it. Giselle reached for Felipe's hand, the gesture simple yet laden with the unspoken words of support she longed to offer.

"Tell me," she said softly. "What have you found? What have you and Daniel been digging into?"

Felipe hesitated, a flicker of frustration crossing his face. "Not as much as I'd hoped." His voice was strained. "Trails gone cold, aliases, the usual . . ." he sighed. "Giselle, tell me about the party, about Karen, about Lotte. That's the missing piece, I think. If there is one."

A flicker of disappointment washed over her, but she pushed it aside. He needed this, the chance to immerse himself once more in the tangible details of their investigation. With renewed determination, Giselle filled them in on the party, how she'd turned potentially revealing conversations on their heads and walked away with a much greater sense that she knew what there was to know about this matronly figure who called herself Lotte.

"And then . . ." she paused.

No sooner had she begun the thought than she felt, beneath several layers of mental and physical exhaustion, a new energy buzzing.

"Something strange happened, something that feels . . . significant, though I couldn't say why."

She hesitated, carefully choosing her words. Felipe leaned forward, his focus homed in on her. It was clear Daniel, too, sensed a pivotal shift. None of them were strangers to the reality that something that just *felt significant* could be the key to everything—even if it took some detective work to figure out why and how. The three of them shared a trust in intuition; it had broken them out of traps and pushed them toward victory in the past.

"Lotte was talking about her past, and her sister. How they were both 'sought-after photographers,' and their boss—well, their 'boss's boss'—found them an apartment in Munich together."

The glaze of intense listening left Daniel's eyes and was replaced, literally in a blink, by blazing interest. He leaned forward forcefully enough to knock a coffee cup askew. It spoke to how seriously she and Felipe took Daniel's "light-bulb moments" that neither of them even glanced at the warm, dark liquid spreading across the tabletop, threatening to drip on the floor.

"Did she say anything else about this boss? Or *his* boss?" That fast, Daniel wore his interrogation face.

Giselle understood how this expression could bring those who'd crossed Daniel to their knees—and, more importantly, to hastily uttered confessions—though she herself had never been intimidated by it. Only spurred on.

"Yeah. That the boss's boss was quite taken with her sister."

"Giselle," he said, his voice low and urgent. "Do you realize what you just said? Do you understand what that could mean?"

"I don't know. That's why I mentioned it. The whole thing seemed so strange, so—" she paused, searching for the right word. "—orchestrated."

Her instincts, always her guiding force, had undoubtedly glowed red over this detail, and she was relieved to see that apparently, she had been onto something.

Daniel stood abruptly. It was a miracle his chair didn't crash against the floor—what a scene his kitchen would have been then: coffee dripping freely from the table, Elena's bags abandoned on the floor in a heap, Daniel's chair flipped on its back during his eureka moment.

"Giselle, that's it!" Daniel said. His tone to express fury and elation sounded nearly the same. In this case, Giselle, Felipe, and even Elena—with no idea what her silly family was on about now—could read in his voice that he felt so gleeful he could have danced.

"Don't you see? It fits—all of it. That's why we haven't found anything on Nils, why his identity is so meticulously hidden. My God . . ." he trailed off.

He turned to Felipe, his face alight as if he stood before a roaring fireplace, while Elena slept on the sofa.

"Hitler's personal photographer, Felipe. It has to be Hoffmann!"

CHAPTER SEVEN

One of the countless forms of manipulation Hitler had used in oiling his way to the top was his propaganda campaign. Daniel remembered looking with chills at the monochrome images of a Hitler who always appeared stone-eyed, manicured, and groomed down to the last detail. He was not so much a man who was always in control, but rather a man desperate for it. He donned every semblance of authority he found and avoided all association with anything he found remotely "weak."

And Heinrich Hoffmann had been the one to snap pictures of him for distribution in Germany and beyond.

He wasn't a monster who orchestrated rallies or penned hate-filled speeches. His evil was far more insidious. Wielding nothing more threatening than a camera, he became one of the chief architects in the rise and dominance of the Nazi machine.

Hoffmann first met Hitler in 1920 after being drawn to the fiery speeches and burgeoning Nazi movement. He'd witnessed what he considered crackling potential, not even in ideology, but—perhaps even more vile—in image. Hitler, with his paintbrush mustache and greasy hair, wasn't exactly a picture of Aryan perfection. Yet, Hoffmann saw a way to sculpt the man, to craft a powerful visual narrative.

He staged photos, placing Hitler in heroic poses amidst cheering crowds, even doctoring images to exaggerate the size of rallies. One of Hoffmann's prized images, used as Nazi propaganda, showed Hitler at the famed Odeonsplatz Square in central Munich, cheering on the outbreak of World War I—the only truly international war to precede the one he himself would catalyze. The image was used, as were many of his; to froth up a national lust for the weaselly Adolf . . . and it was a fake.

Hoffmann wasn't a chronicler; he was a propagandist, weaving a web of lies through calculated snapshots. These images flooded newspapers and homes, and a fringe politician blossomed into a charismatic leader.

Their bond wasn't just professional. As a craven sycophant, Hoffmann reveled in Hitler's approval. When Hitler banned anyone else from taking his picture, Hoffmann had the ridiculous honor of being his official photographer. He was no less pleased than Cinderella watching the prince slide a just-right slipper on her foot while the kingdom's other maidens watched on with envy. He fawned over the man's every whim, fueling Hitler's growing narcissism.

This toxic partnership reached a critical pitch in 1932. Enter Eva Braun, a young woman with aspirations of becoming a photographer. Fate, or perhaps Hoffmann's twisted sense of amusement, landed her a position at his studio. Ambitious but perhaps a touch naive, Eva saw Hitler as a political powerhouse and—still in a dark, a mysterious way a man to be won.

In her was an opportunist who saw a chance to further solidify Hoffmann's position. He "introduced" Eva to Hitler, no doubt relishing the power play. Despite Eva's initial flirtations, Hitler wasn't immediately smitten. He found her attractive, yes, but a serious relationship wasn't part of his grand plan—not to mention she went against the grain of his preference that women be seen and not heard.

Eva, however, was relentless. She used her position at Hoffmann's studio to her advantage, "crossing paths" with Hitler as her youthful infatuation morphed into something more of an obsessive pursuit fueled by a misplaced sense of belonging.

Over time, Hitler succumbed to her persistence, perhaps out of loneliness, perhaps to quell rumors about his sexuality. Or perhaps—as Daniel roared in the midst of regaling Felipe and Giselle with Heinrich's backstory—to make it due Hitler's fragile ego for getting rejected by art school all those years before.

By any account, the relationship that first germinated within the walls of Hoffmann's propaganda studio supplied the Nazi arsenal with another weapon: a "perfect Aryan woman" to accompany Hitler, and just as importantly, to be photographed with him.

CHAPTER EIGHT

Felipe watched Giselle lean back, her eyes narrowed in thought. In that moment, she looked every bit herself again: the Giselle who never backs down from any challenge. Next to him, Daniel was hunched over his computer, likely confirming their suspicions with his own channels. Amidst the buzzing of their investigation, Felipe's mind finally settled.

"Nils just dropped the extra 'n'," Daniel blurted out, more to himself than anyone else. This was how it felt for a puzzle piece to finally click with a horrifying certainty. "Hoffmann. Not Braun or Hitler, but an extension . . ."

Felipe and Giselle nodded, silently taking it all in.

This was their break. Nils wasn't some unrelated boy; he was heir to the legacy of the Führer's deception, and therefore very likely the closest thing Adolf Hitler had to a son.

Felipe experienced relief down to his dangling fingertips. This was no crumb. He looked toward Daniel's living room, where Elena had fallen asleep in front of the TV, curled in a ball like a cat, and the world shifted on its axis. All this, all their single-minded pursuit, was for her. To carve a sliver of safety and certainty out of a past that bled into their present.

That evening, with Elena finally asleep in one of Daniel's guest rooms, Felipe and Giselle lay awake in the quiet. It wasn't the passionate reunion he'd craved, but the conversation was different somehow. They spoke of Elena's first words, her fearless toddling, weaving mundane memories into the tapestry of their extraordinary lives. Perhaps, for right now, this was even better than making love all night.

It was reclaiming a piece of the ordinary.

~~~

Glancing through the cracked door of his guest bedroom, Daniel experienced a familiar twisting feeling in his gut as he briefly saw them. His loved ones' happy whispers, shared smiles, the simple act of holding hands across the sheets— these were moments he clung to, even though they reminded him of all he'd lost.

His thoughts returned to Paraguay, to his sons nearly snatched away forever by deluded indoctrination. He knew, the way Felipe knew, that once you've stared into that abyss, you can never fully walk away. Theirs was a fight against an echo, and it was a fight that might never truly be won.

CHAPTER NINE

Colonel Judd loved the smell of the potting shed first thing in the morning. The earthy scents of damp soil and sprouting green shoots were better than any cup of coffee. Of course, he still enjoyed his strong brew from the antique French press he had purchased on a trip to Paris years ago. But the garden . . . that was where his heart sang these days.

He carefully arranged a new tray of lettuce seedlings on the potting bench. The New England sun was strong even early in the morning. When he saw his wife's pleasant, smiling face under her wide-brimmed straw hat, he assumed she was making the usual rounds to inquire about his Swiss chard and asparagus.

This time, she was here to tell him, "Your favorite vigilante is on the phone."

Inside his home office, before he'd even received a proper hello, Judd heard, "I've got a break in this Karen Fegel business. Need your help." After all these years, it still amused Judd how his old comrade never ceased to skip the pleasantries.

"Let's hear it."

"No lectures on how to grow kale today?"

Judd let out a chuckle, unruffled. "What can I tell you? Its hardiness is perfect for the topography here. Grow the stuff all goddamn year."

"Sounds like a dream."

Through the line came the distinct sound of the last drops of bourbon being drained from a glass, the ice cubes clinking against Daniel's teeth.

Judd pressed a fingertip into the soil to check its moisture level. It was springy, the perfect level of dampness.

"I'm not kidding you, Daniel. It'll muscle through outside long as you're two weeks off the last frost. Not that you'd *start* it outside. One damn thing about this place: growing season's too short. Gotta seed your kale inside for starters."

"Alright, alright," Daniel said. "So, I've got a champagne flute that may have a set of prints."

From there, Daniel told Judd the details: Giselle and the birthday party for Lotte, Karen's mail, and Lotte's discarded glass, Lotte and her sister taking pictures for a man presumed to be the image-maker of Hitler himself. Nils almost certainly being Heinrich Hoffmann's son. Daniel shook his head quietly as he reported this last bit, still unable to fully process it himself.

Judd imagined Daniel in his luxurious apartment overlooking the lake, pacing back and forth in agitation. He knew how long Daniel had been chasing this ghost, the burning desire for justice fueling him. For years it had consumed Judd too, and he knew how easily it could return.

And make no mistake—Judd applauded Daniel, along with Felipe and Giselle, for everything they were doing. When the stakes were as high as Hitler running free or being thrown in a cage (or a grave, for all Judd cared), nearly anything was justified. Daniel went to the lengths he had to. He and Felipe gave up sleep until they were bleary enough that the world looked smeared with Vaseline. Still, there came a point—as Judd had learned all too personally—when you had to detach, know you'd done all you could to stanch the evil, and just live your life.

Judd knew Daniel didn't have that part down, and some-times he worried he never would.

He could certainly understand it. How Daniel reasoned that staying on high alert every moment of his long nights—at least when he didn't have weekends with his boys and wasn't armchair-coaching a football match—was necessary in a world Hitler still saw as his for the taking. But it was a disas-trous thing to loiter in hypervigilance too long, perpetually listening to the voice in your head that says you aren't safe and neither are your loved ones. Judd glanced up at his wife, watering her flower bed and smiling over at him. She was why he'd come this far away from it all. Not physically. He could still zip off to New York for necessary work without incurring the sense that he'd really left home at all. But he'd not only greatly decreased his involvement in that type of activity alto-gether; he'd learned the art of concealing concerns whenever he crossed the threshold from that life to home life.

And if ever that particular demarcation didn't do the trick, walking through his garden gate did.

As much as he wished he could convince Daniel of the merits of, to a certain extent, dismissing the pains and wor-ries, Judd knew he'd have to settle for applying it in his own life. He hoped that one day Daniel would find a work-life bal-ance, an Everest of a challenge for a former Mossad agent. He could even serve as a model for Felipe.

"Yes," Judd said finally, coming back to the present. "I can look into the prints for you. They still owe me plenty of favors at Langley. But Daniel—"

Judd ran his fingers along the rough wooden edge of the workbench. He'd need to handle this carefully. The last thing he wanted was for Daniel and his associates to rush in head-first, potentially alerting their target and blowing their cover. He knew that on a normal basis, Daniel was a cool-headed leader with a steady trigger finger, but he also knew the man's impatience. Particularly in any situation where his family was—or perceived to be—in danger.

"What is it?" Daniel grumbled impatiently.

"Be cautious," Judd said gently, in the voice he used when he talked to his own grown son about important life decisions. "It sounds like you've got something real. And you've got something traceable at this point. But wait for me to trace it properly and come back to you with real answers before you leap. Because mark my words, Daniel, you cannot get anything wrong when accusing people of Nazi involvement. No matter how certain you are . . . no matter that you have all the right reasons for wanting to barrel ahead, be patient."

He slowed down and breathed.

"If you get it *even a little bit* wrong, you lose your chance at shutting the monster down."

CHAPTER TEN

The afternoon sun cast long shadows across the wide boulevard as Felipe and Daniel staked out a discreet vantage point across the street. The café they chose bustled with mid-afternoon patrons, a noisy symphony of clinking cups and snippets of overheard conversation. It offered the perfect cover. From their corner table, they had an unobstructed view of an apartment building with a gleaming façade.

"Typical," Felipe muttered, studying the building through narrowed eyes. "Obscene wealth hiding in plain sight."

Daniel, hunched over a lukewarm espresso, grunted in agreement. "They wouldn't choose anything too flashy. Blending in is the whole point."

The building, a six-story block of pale brick and expansive windows, seemed unremarkable at first glance. Yet, a closer look revealed subtle tells. Security cameras perched discreetly above the entrance; their unblinking lenses tucked beneath stylish awnings. The garden in the back, visible from their vantage point, was manicured to the point of being devoid of the joyful untidiness that usually accompanied communal spaces. This wasn't a place built for casual chats with neighbors; it was a fortress disguised as a home.

"Two apartments per floor, maybe three," Felipe murmured. "What do you want to bet the penthouse is Lotte's? Taking up the whole floor."

"Space enough for a whole brood," Daniel said, the thought leaving a sour taste in his mouth. The idea of another generation of Hitlers or Brauns hiding within those walls made his blood run cold.

They watched as a sleek black Mercedes slid into the alley leading to the underground garage, its tinted windows obscuring the driver. Felipe jotted down the license plate number, adding another thread to their growing web of evidence.

"Someone important, or someone with something to hide," he mused aloud.

"Probably both," Daniel replied.

The day stretched into evening, and the two men took shifts, nursed lukewarm coffees, and pretended to show interest in the newspapers spread out before them. Their patience was rewarded. Against the sky's last rays of sun, a single window on the top floor of the building glowed with warm light.

"There she is," Felipe said quietly. The sight of that illuminated window, a beacon in the anonymity of the building, filled him with a strange mixture of rage and grim satisfaction.

"Let's see who else is around," Daniel suggested, reaching for his binoculars. Systematically, he swept across the building's facade, floor by floor. Several windows remained dark, their occupants either absent or keeping to the shadows. On the fourth floor, a flicker of movement caught his eye. A figure hunched by the window, quickly drawing the curtains shut as if sensing their scrutiny.

"Fourth floor, right side," Daniel said, keeping his voice low. "Someone just shut their curtains in a hurry."

Felipe leaned forward, energized by the thrill of the hunt.

"Another one of them? A lookout?" He imagined a network of collaborators, each considering themselves honored to volunteer as security detail for Gretl Braun.

In the waning daylight, they cataloged comings and goings: a young couple projecting laughter onto the street, a delivery man carrying a crate of wine, and a middle-aged woman returning home with a bulging grocery bag. All seemingly ordinary lives brushing up against extraordinary evil.

As the clock struck midnight, Felipe stretched, his body stiff from hours seated in the uncomfortable chair at the café.

"Time to call it a night," he said reluctantly.

Daniel nodded. "For now. We need those blueprints so we can find out what's behind those walls."

Outside the café, they blended in perfectly with the thinning crowd. As they walked, Felipe couldn't shake the image of that single illuminated window, the unsettling knowledge that somewhere within that building, a ghost of the past lingered, waiting to be exorcised.

~~~

Buenos Aires' municipal planning department was a labyrinth of faded grandeur and bureaucratic inertia. Musty files stacked in towering columns lined dimly lit corridors, the rhythmic tapping of typewriters creating a strange percussive symphony against the whispers of waiting clerks. It was here, amidst the city's well-documented past, that Felipe hoped to unearth the truth about the modern apartment building that seemed to defy history.

Through a carefully cultivated mix of charm, half-truths, and discreetly slipped pesos, he found himself hunched over a cracked wooden desk, and a sour-faced clerk reluctantly produced the requested files with a huff of disapproval. As the architectural plans unfurled before him, a sense of triumph flared within him. This was progress—a tangible clue in a sea of whispered suspicions and dead-ends.

The building, confirmed to have been constructed in 1960, was a testament to that era's embrace of clean lines and understated luxury. The plans revealed generously proportioned apartments, each with ample living spaces, modern kitchens, and multiple bedrooms. The top floor penthouse, undoubtedly Lotte's territory, spoke of unchecked wealth and privilege. A private elevator whisked the building's residents directly into the entry hall of their own apartments, ensuring privacy and isolation.

As Felipe traced his finger along the lines representing expansive living rooms and opulent bedrooms, he tried to calm himself of the resentment he felt flare up. His own apartment, a charming older space filled with Giselle's laughter and Elena's bright chatter, had become a battleground. Each crack in the plaster seemed to symbolize a dead end in their search, each cramped corner a reminder of the threat looming over their fragile sense of peace. The echoes of sleepless nights and whispered fears clung to the familiar rooms, tainting the very idea of home.

The discovery that a German bank was the true owner of Lotte's apartment building was both unsurprising and deeply unsettling. The attached property management company, with its conveniently located storefront, seemed almost too convenient to be true, but Felipe was looking at it in writing. The multifaceted real estate company held the key, quite literally, to the fortress that loomed over it.

He couldn't help imagining a different apartment for himself and his family. Something fresh, untouched by the shadows of the past. His mind wandered to sun-drenched spaces in another part of the city, far removed from this tainted neighborhood. Perhaps a larger space with a room painted in Elena's favorite shade of yellow—a space where the laughter wouldn't compete with ghosts that stalked their current dwelling.

An image of Giselle, her smile radiating contentment as she moved about this hypothetical new home, populated vividly in his mind's eye. He longed to see her settled somewhere she could light up regularly, like she had when they were newly married. Before a relentless monster chase had taken over their lives.

The thought expanded, bolder and brighter. Another bedroom, a tiny nursery filled with soft colors and a gentle rocking chair . . . a fresh start, not just in a new space, but with a growing family. Giselle's quiet yearning for another child echoed in his own heart. It wasn't anything he could say out loud to her yet. He had to be certain he could withstand the idea of bringing another child into this world, and he knew as well as Giselle that he wouldn't commit to the feeling until *this world* had done its part to change.

The world that would see him have another child was a world post-Hitler.

He allowed his mind to drift.

. . . *maybe even Geneva*, he thought. A haven near Daniel, potentially offering shared meals and genuine family laughter.

He blinked, refocusing on the plans spread out before him. There was work to be done, history to untangle. He challenged himself to look at a cozy future as a reward to be won rather than a distraction to indulge. With that, Felipe returned his attention to the task at hand, resolved to dismantle the fortress of secrets brick by brick.

~~~

The moment Daniel stepped into the building's lobby, reflective because of the morning sun, he registered that the air hung heavy with a coolness that went beyond mere air-conditioning; it was a calculated detachment meant to intimidate.

The space was all gleaming marble and polished wood, reminiscent of a bank more than an apartment lobby. Behind an imposing wooden desk sat a severe-looking man with short, dark hair and a moustache trimmed so perfectly that it appeared unnatural. His suit was impeccably pressed, his posture ramrod straight. He carried the unmistakable air of a former soldier. And he spoke only German.

Adopting the nearest thing he had to an innocent expression, Daniel approached the desk. Speaking in purposefully mangled German laced with just enough of a Spanish accent to hint at foreign origins, he inquired about possible vacancies in the building.

The response was curt, dismissive: "No openings."

No further information was offered. Despite his attempts to appear as a wealthy retiree seeking a change of pace, the man's expression remained unchanged.

"Surely there may be something in the near future," Daniel pressed. His eyes darted over the empty lobby, seeking any sign of life beyond this unyielding gatekeeper.

The man's lips thinned in a tight smile that didn't reach his eyes. Without a word, he reached beneath his desk and pressed a discreetly placed button. From a side door, a younger, broader man emerged, with a poorly concealed bulge beneath his ill-fitted jacket. Another ex-military type, Daniel surmised. The muscle to back up the first man's authority.

With a stoic gesture toward the exit, the silent enforcer invited Daniel to leave the premises without explanation, without the need to explain anything to someone who was not "one of them."

Daniel tempered the anger that surged with him by chanting to himself a reminder that escalating the situation would gain him nothing. He retreated with feigned nonchalance, but his every sense was on high alert. As he stepped back onto the bustling street, he cast one last glance over his shoulder. The clerk's eyes did not leave the confines of his silhouette.

Luckily, nothing about the success of the mission depended on cooperation from an apartment building clerk with his nose in the air. Nearby sat the property management company—Daniel's next stop.

A far cry from the austere lobby he'd just left—or, more accurately, escorted from—this place was light and airy. Photos of condos, each promising a slice of sun-drenched luxury, gleamed along the walls. A woman with a tidy blonde bob and a smile of plastic sweetness greeted him from behind the reception desk.

Daniel recited his story just as he had planned; the tale of a soon-to-be-retiree with a desire for a quieter life, yet still within the embrace of the city. As he spoke, his eyes scanned the office. Three desks lined an open area that narrowed into a corridor, presumably leading to additional offices in the back. Under the guise of gawking in awe at the property photos, he discreetly tested the weight of the reception room door—light, secured by a simple lock.

"Allow me to check our listings," the woman replied. Despite her unwavering smile, Daniel knew a stalling tactic when he saw one. No doubt she was sizing him up to determine if he was a legitimate client or . . . well, exactly who and what he was. A spy. Someone who was onto the possible fishiness of the enterprise and intended to bring it down.

A request to use the restroom was met with a finger pointed toward the back corridor and nothing more. But he could feel the woman's gaze on his retreating back. He stopped at the first office door, listening for any voices inside. Nothing. Same with the second. A small kitchenette, a restroom, and finally, at the very end, another closed door.

The temptation to open it was strong. Yet, something about the silence of the office and the watchful eyes of the receptionist held him back. Now wasn't the time for risks. Today was only about collecting landmarks for the mental map he would use when he came back later, under the cover of darkness.

Back at the reception desk, the woman shook her head apologetically. "Unfortunately, sir, we have nothing in that specific area at the moment."

Her tone made it clear that the conversation was over.

~~~

Back at Giselle and Felipe's apartment, a warm light spilled out into the falling darkness as they gathered around the kitchen table. Oblivious to the undercurrent of seriousness running through her home, Elena hummed tunelessly as she built a castle out of mismatched blocks.

Felipe went first in this odd show-and-tell they'd all grown accustomed to. He unrolled blueprints chock full of crisp lines and, with practiced ease, outlined what he'd uncovered about the building. "It was built in 1960, likely with a significant influx of money. That fits the timeline of their escape."

He kept his voice programmed to a clinical tone, which made talking about all of this easier somehow. Plus, he knew his "work voice" was boring to Elena and therefore wouldn't attract her attention to the grim matters they sat dissecting at the kitchen table.

Daniel grunted his agreement. "They have muscle guarding the front, and Lord knows what else is hidden inside. And the management company was tight-lipped. These people aren't merely hiding—they're entrenched."

Giselle absorbed the information as clinically as Felipe spoke. The pieces fit. To a certain extent, it was all math.

"Entrenched is a good word for them," she murmured. Her eyes strayed to where Elena placed a tiny plastic flag atop her block fortress. "Not to mention clannish. They monitor each other to a startling degree."

Felipe met her eyes with interest. "Did you find something out?"

In a mellow voice, Giselle told them what she had heard standing outside Karen's apartment that afternoon, and how her conversation with Karen had gone afterwards. Felipe responded to her story in the way she had expected: he found it encouraging news for their case—if bad news for the state of college campuses and the world in general—but he otherwise remained as subdued as Giselle herself.

Daniel, on the other hand, nodded with an enthusiastic pensiveness, appearing to have heard more than she believed she had recounted. Annoyed by this to a certain degree, she said, "Uncle Daniel, for goodness' sake, I can't see any relevance of all this. Lotte—Gretl—used her influence to make sure nothing will ever happen to Nils."

"So, no clue as to which paper?" Felipe asked gently.

Giselle shook her head. "And I'd look suspicious to press anymore." She did not add that she was increasingly concerned she had already pressed too hard. That was a risk at every turn of this investigation, but today she heard the fear of being exposed in Karen's voice when she had ended the call to avoid Giselle's last question, not even coming up with a viable excuse for her departure.

Giselle didn't tell her husband and uncle about the pit in her stomach that testified to the likelihood that she might have alienated Karen for good.

"So, the picture won't actually be printed," Daniel said casually. "That doesn't mean it's useless information for us." Giselle was about to object that she thought that's exactly what it meant when Daniel continued: "It might still exist. What if we could find it?"

Felipe's head tilted at the sound of a block castle crumbling in the living room. "Do you really think there's any chance Gretl wouldn't demand to see both the print and negative destroyed?"

With a shrug, Daniel said, "I don't know that we need the actual picture. We need—"

"—the editor who agreed not to print it," Giselle jumped in. She took a long sip of lukewarm coffee, feeling it slightly enliven her spirit.

A tight smile paused on Daniel's lips; an indication he was glad to see her appear more hopeful. "Exactly."

"But how would we get an editor on board?" Felipe wondered aloud. He denounced the route they had taken in learning more about Lotte and Nils's apartment building. It was one thing to bribe a mail carrier—it was quite another to pay off a high-level member of the press. One, it would probably take a great deal more, and two, no one particularly wanted to see Daniel lose his wealth bribing a host of unofficial witnesses. Besides, editors at some papers would be loath to forgo their professional ethics for an unexpected payday: many of them would feel protective of their illustrious careers, present and future.

"So, how would we win them over?" Felipe reiterated.

Giselle and Daniel both gazed at him thoughtfully. Daniel was first to crack a smile, indicative of the fact that, as always, he had a plan.

~~~

The trilling of the telephone cut through their conversation.

It was Karen, full of nervous excitement, brimming with news.

With so much happening, a wedding had been hastily planned.

"It's going to be small!" she rushed to tell Giselle in a way that made Giselle think she'd rehearsed this reassurance several times already—likely for relatives aghast that a sudden wedding might rob the bride of all the pomp and circumstance a proper wedding day deserved.

"A quick ceremony while I can still fit in my dress." Her voice turned hesitant as she reached the point of her call. "Giselle, I know it's a lot to ask, but . . . would you be one of my bridesmaids?"

The request hung in the air, bright and heavy at the same time. It represented the sort of contradiction Giselle found she was growing accustomed to; a golden opportunity, in terms of their investigation and hunt, that nonetheless left her sick to her stomach. It was one thing to stalk from the shadows, to dissect birth certificates and architectural plans; it was quite another to smile and hold a bouquet, to pretend to be joyful for a woman who could very well be the niece of Eva Braun.

It was the type of contradiction Giselle was getting used to: a valuable opportunity for their investigation and hunt, one that still made her uneasy.

She knew she had to answer quickly, so she breathed her way through the battle between her investigative instincts and a lingering sense of guilt. Karen, for all her naivete, hadn't been cruel; she was a woman swept up in a monstrous legacy—she wasn't its architect.

She wasn't even its chronicler. Or his child.

"Yes," she heard herself say. "Of course, Karen. I'd be honored."

The relief in Karen's voice was almost unbearable. She hung up with a trembling hand.

Across the table, Felipe and Daniel exchanged a glance that either spelled concern for Giselle or excitement over what another call from Karen meant—maybe both.

"This is good, Giselle," Felipe said gently after she told them the latest. "It could be the break we need."

Daniel nodded, but otherwise he remained quiet. They both knew that the line Giselle walked was perilously thin. They needed her to get close, to gather information, but not at the cost of her own well-being. It was starting to take a toll on her that neither of them could ignore.

Staring at the blueprints shuffled across the table and the scattered fragments of Elena's block castle, Giselle felt adrift. Each step they took forward was one step deeper into a moral quagmire. She was becoming a spy, a deceiver, all in the name of a truth that might never bring the peace they so desperately craved.

CHAPTER ELEVEN

Giselle entered the small, nondescript building housing *El Argentino Liberal*, a fledgling newspaper that still bore the excitement and messiness of a start-up operation. The sharp smell of fresh ink, dusty paper, and cheap coffee filled the air as she stepped past the bustling reception area, where a lone secretary was pounding away at a typewriter between brushing stray curls back from her face.

The office itself was cramped and simple. Piles of newspapers were scattered across desks, and workers moved about with an almost frenetic energy, their faces flushed with the purpose of trying to prove they belonged in the same city that housed much larger, more established publications.

Buenos Aires itself buzzed beyond the office windows, alive with the heat and rhythm of the afternoon. The constant hum of cars in the street below mixed with the cacophony of voices spilling out from cafés and the scent of grilled meat wafting in from a nearby parrilla. There was no escaping the pulse of this city, a place where old-world charm and the embers of revolution coexisted in every corner.

As Giselle made her way down a narrow hallway, she was well aware of how much she stood out. She wasn't just another worker at the office—she was a young woman in elegant but simple attire: a cream-colored blouse with delicate buttons paired with a pencil skirt, and her long, dark hair fell in soft waves over her shoulders. She caught the glances of a few passing workers and responded with a composed smile, walking with the air of someone who had been in newsrooms like this a hundred times before.

Finally, she reached the door marked *Editor: Agustin Pérez*. She paused briefly. The plan was simple enough: appeal to his pride, stroke his ego, and walk away with whatever he may have on Nils Hoffman. And yet, Giselle could feel the weight of her task.

This wasn't just an interview—it was a delicate dance on the edge of danger.

This wasn't just an interview—it was a risky encounter.

She knocked lightly, hearing a shuffle of papers before a soft voice called, "Come in."

Giselle entered, closing the door gently behind her. Even standing up, Agustin Pérez's head barely peeked over the mountain of papers on his small wooden desk. The team had done their research on him, of course, but here he was in the flesh. Early thirties with shy brown eyes hidden behind large, wire-rimmed glasses, his thin frame seeming to fold in on itself as he rose awkwardly to greet her.

"Señorita Dubois, is it?" he asked in hesitant Spanish, his voice gentle, tentative.

"Yes," Giselle said smoothly, offering her hand with a warm smile. "Marianne Dubois. *L'Éclat Suisse* in Geneva. Thank you for agreeing to meet with me, Señor Pérez."

Agustin blushed slightly as he shook her hand, fumbling with his glasses before returning to his seat. "Please, sit. I'm honored that you've come all the way here . . . and from Geneva, you said?"

"Indeed," Giselle replied, her voice taking on a soft French accent as she sat down opposite him, carefully crossing her legs and folding her hands in her lap. "We are working on a special section about individuals around the world who have stood up to Nazism. Argentina is of particular interest to us because—as you know, like Switzerland—it remained neutral during the war, despite being deeply affected by its horrors."

Agustin nodded slowly. "Yes, Argentina is . . . complex in that way."

"It is," Giselle agreed, her voice a soothing melody of reassurance. "But we've received a tip that your young paper has been doing extraordinary work in exposing Nazi activity here in Buenos Aires, especially among the German Expat community."

Agustin's eyes widened in surprise. "You've heard about our work?"

"Yes," she said with a conspiratorial smile. "I've read what you've printed so far, and it's impressive. But . . ." she leaned in slightly and lowered her voice, "I am curious if you have any unpublished material. Sometimes the bravest work is what gets left out of the papers."

The color rose in Agustin's cheeks, and he straightened up in his chair. Giselle could see the flicker of pride in his eyes, the excitement of being acknowledged by a prestigious international magazine—and the glossy-haired, silken-voiced journalist who represented it.

"Well," Agustin began, stumbling over his words as he grew more animated, "we have been . . . cautious with some of our material. You see, it's a dangerous topic. There are still powerful people in the German community here, and—"

"And threats have been made?" Giselle finished for him, tilting her head in sympathy.

Agustin nodded, his face serious. "Yes, in fact, we recently chose not to run a story after some . . . legal threats. But it's more than just that. I've had my reporters digging deeper, and we've uncovered some things that . . ." He trailed off, his eyes darting nervously to the door.

Giselle kept her expression calm, but her heart quickened with anticipation.

"Agustin, I understand how difficult it must be for a paper like yours to navigate these waters. But we at *L'Éclat Suisse* believe that stories like yours—stories of courage in the face of danger—need to be told. The world needs to know what's happening here."

She watched as Agustin's hesitation began to melt under the warmth of her praise. After a brief pause, he stood abruptly and walked over to a filing cabinet in the corner of his office. Giselle's heart pounded in her chest as she watched him rummage through the drawers, finally pulling out a small reel-to-reel tape. He placed it on the desk with slightly trembling hands.

"We sent a reporter to one of the universities a few weeks ago," he explained. "There were rumors of Nazi gatherings on campus, so we had him pose as a student and secretly record one of their meetings. We haven't run the story yet . . . it's . . . too dangerous."

Giselle's eyes widened, though she kept her face neutral. "And you obtained a clear recording of that meeting?"

Agustin nodded quickly, his fingers fumbling with the reel as he set it up on a small tape recorder. "I think . . . I think you'll find it interesting. This is the kind of evidence that could make a real difference."

The weight of the moment pressed down on Giselle as the tape began to whirr softly. The recording crackled to life, the sound of shuffling feet and muted voices echoing from the player. Then, slowly, the voices grew clearer. The conversation shifted from mundane chatter to something far darker.

". . . and as we all know, Herr Hitler was a visionary," a male voice said, his tone dripping with reverence. "It is our duty to ensure that his message lives on, that it spreads to a new generation of soldiers willing to fight for the Reich."

Another voice chimed in from an even younger-sounding man. "We have an opportunity here in Buenos Aires. The world has forgotten us, but we will rise again. We are the future."

Giselle felt a chill creep down her spine as the voices continued, their words filled with venom and an almost religious fervor. They spoke of Hitler as a messiah, of his vision as something to be revered and resurrected.

"We are not just students," the first voice continued. "We are soldiers of the Reich. We will take this message beyond the borders of Argentina. We will find others like us—young men and women who believe in the purity of the German race—who believe in our mission."

Giselle clenched her fists in her lap. The room felt suddenly colder despite the oppressive heat outside. The voices on the tape were so casual, so confident in their hatred. It was as though the war had never ended for them—its poison still festered, waiting for the right moment to spread again.

Agustin turned off the tape and looked at Giselle, his face pale with uncertainty.

"This . . . this is what we're up against," he whispered, his voice trembling slightly. "I don't know how much longer we can keep this quiet."

With a deep breath, Giselle forced herself to remain composed despite the storm of emotions inside her. She made sure her smile at Agustin reflected admiration and understanding. "This is incredible work, Agustin. Dangerous, yes—but important. The world needs to hear this."

Agustin looked at her with wide eyes, his uncertainty beginning to melt into something more resolute. "Do you think . . . do you think it could make a difference?"

"I do," Giselle said firmly. In that moment, there was nothing of Marianne Dubois in her tone or in her thoughts. She appreciated this young editor for battling his own prolific nerves— not to mention the ambivalence of his home country—to take on the resurfacing of this plague.

"This could expose them for what they are before they have a chance to grow any stronger."

Agustin sat back in his chair, letting out a long breath as if a weight had been lifted from him.

"Then . . . then maybe it's time we published it. If people like you are willing to stand up against them . . . maybe we can, too."

Giselle smiled warmly, though inside she felt the cold grip of fear. This was bigger than they had realized. The Nazi flame hadn't just flickered back to life—it was threatening to spread. And they had to extinguish it before it consumed everything.

"Thank you for sharing this with me," she said softly, standing and offering him her hand once more. "You are very brave, Agustin. I will make sure the world knows it."

As she left the office and stepped back into the humid Buenos Aires streets, the weight of what she had heard settled on her like an iron mantle. She hurriedly slipped into a nearby café, the noise of the city fading as she made her way inside.

~~~

As Daniel walked briskly through the wide streets, his polished shoes slapped the cobblestone with every step. The sun was directly overhead at noon, shining on the buildings' decorative exteriors. The capital was alive with its usual frenetic energy—cars honking, vendors calling out in rapid Spanish, the aroma of sizzling empanadas mingling with the city's ever-present scent of gasoline.

But Daniel's mind was elsewhere, focused sharply on the task at hand. He straightened his jacket, the fabric snug against his broad shoulders, and adjusted his fedora as he approached the headquarters of *El Sensacional*, one of the largest and most widely read newspapers in Buenos Aires. Unlike the more serious, esteemed publications, *El Sensacional* was known for its tendency to blur the line between fact and scandal, between hard news and idle gossip. But its reach was undeniable.

Daniel rolled his eyes as he stepped into a lobby full of glossy marble floors reflecting the art-deco fixtures that had seen better days. A receptionist behind the desk looked up briefly, uninterested in yet another visitor, before returning to her magazine.

"Señor Lavy, here to see Gael Fernandez," he said in perfect, clipped Spanish.

A curt nod followed as she waved him through. Daniel strolled past the front desk and into the bustling office space beyond. The building had the unmistakable smell of fresh ink and cigarette smoke. Phones rang, reporters shouted, and typewriters clattered furiously as the day's stories took form. There was a nervous energy here, an atmosphere full of people desperate to stay relevant, to break the next big story, even if it meant tearing others down to do it.

At the far end of the room, Daniel spotted a large office door adorned with a gold plaque reading *Editor: Gael Fernandez*. He knocked twice and entered without waiting for a response.

Inside, Gael Fernandez sat behind an oversized desk littered with paper, magazines, and a half-eaten sandwich. He cut an unimpressive figure—his bulbous belly stretched his shirt taut, and his thinning hair was slicked back in a futile attempt to hide his balding crown. But it was evident that Gael didn't care about his appearance—his eyes glittered with the kind of hunger Daniel had seen in many men before. The kind of hunger that could make a man powerful in all the wrong ways.

Gael looked up from a stack of papers, his gaze landing on Daniel with curiosity. "Señor Lavy, is it?"

"Yes." Daniel strode across the room to extend his hand with unmistakable confidence. "Thank you for seeing me on such short notice."

Gael accepted the gesture with a clammy hand, which then motioned for Daniel to sit. Daniel took a seat in one of the plush leather chairs across from the desk, his eyes scanning the office.

It was as gaudy as he'd imagined—a shrine to celebrity culture. Movie posters and autographed photos lined the walls, featuring both Argentine and American film stars. He noted a particularly large, framed photograph of Marlene Dietrich and couldn't help the small smirk that tugged at the corner of his mouth.

"You have a taste for the glamorous life, I see," Daniel said, nodding to the memorabilia.

Gael's chest actually puffed up slightly with the recognition.

"Ah, yes. I've always been a fan of cinema—Hollywood, Europe, even a few of our local stars. It's a way to connect with the world, you know? To see beyond this city."

"I understand completely," Daniel replied. "I can tell you've cultivated a passion here. That sort of dedication is rare."

Gael's eyes gleamed at the compliment. His shoulders relaxed back into his swivel chair. "What brings you here today, Señor Lavy? You mentioned something about a sensitive matter?"

Daniel's pause purposefully gave Gael a moment to bask in the small glow of importance. He could already tell that this man thrived on feeling like he had access to a world of secrets—something bigger than the blasé gossip of the city. And so, Daniel gave him what he craved.

"I'm here on behalf of a German film star," Daniel began, his voice taking on a measured, deliberate tone. "Her son is . . . let's just say, not where he ought to be. He's been involved in some unsavory activities while studying at a university here in Buenos Aires."

Gael's brow furrowed in confusion. "A German film star? Who?"

Daniel leaned forward slightly, lowering his voice. "I'm not at liberty to say . . . not yet, anyway. It's still under wraps. But I've been hired to locate the boy and handle the situation discreetly before it becomes a scandal."

Gael couldn't prevent his hand from twitching toward a pen and notepad, as though preparing to scribble down every tantalizing detail. "And what does this have to do with *El Sensacional*?"

Daniel smiled faintly.

"I believe one of the papers in this city captured a photo of him during one of these protests. You can imagine the damage such an image could cause—both to his mother's career and the boy's future."

Gael shifted in his seat, his eyes narrowing slightly. "So, you're looking for these photos. You think I have them?"

"I do," Daniel said calmly. "I've heard rumors that your paper might have obtained a few photos during the protests—images of certain individuals who should remain . . . anonymous, for now."

Gael let out a soft chuckle, the sound oily and self-satisfied. "Photos of a German film star's son, involved in protests? That sounds scandalous indeed."

Daniel observed Gael's reaction with curiosity on one hand and repulsion on the other.

"If you have them, Señor Fernandez, I'm prepared to offer something in exchange. Though, I doubt money is what you're after."

Gael's eyes lit up with an anticipation indistinguishable from outright greed. "You're right about that. I'm not particularly interested in money, not when I could get something far more valuable. What are you offering?"

Daniel paused, letting the moment stretch out. He let his gaze sweep around the room again, taking in the posters and autographed photos before locking eyes with Gael.

"An exclusive interview. I could arrange for your paper to be the first to interview my client about the rumors surrounding her recent affair with her costar."

Gael's breath hitched. He leaned forward, and his chair creaked. He tapped the pen to his desk rapidly. "Her affair? With whom? Who are we talking about?"

Daniel smiled slightly.

"I can't say just yet. But you know how these things go—rumors spread like wildfire in the film industry. It could be any number of famous names. But if you're interested, I could make sure *El Sensacional* gets the scoop."

Gael's eyes practically glowed with excitement. He muttered a few names under his breath, trying to piece together the puzzle. "Hildegard? Or maybe . . . Dietrich? No, no . . . someone younger . . ."

Daniel played his part expertly, keeping his expression carefully neutral, only allowing the occasional glimmer of amusement to cross his face. He watched the editor tie his own imagination into knots. He didn't even need to nudge him further—the bait had been set, and Gael had taken it eagerly.

"I might be able to arrange something . . . but only if I get those photos," Daniel said softly.

Gael nodded quickly, practically vibrating with excitement. "Of course, of course! Let me see what we have . . ."

He stood up from his desk and crossed the room to a large filing cabinet tucked away in the corner. As he rifled through folders, Daniel sat back in his chair, maintaining an outward calmness despite the quickening pace of his pulse. If this worked, if Gael truly had more photos of the young Nazi sympathizers . . .

Finally, Gael pulled out a manila folder, which he brought over to the desk and laid open before Daniel with no small amount of flourish. Inside were a dozen or more glossy black-and-white photographs. Daniel's heart skipped a beat as he saw the images—groups of young men and women, mostly in their late teens or early twenties, gathered at a protest. Some were caught mid-chant and others held signs, their expressions defiant.

He saw faces he wished he could recognize—faces that could be key players in the new wave of Nazi activity spreading through Buenos Aires. Nils Hoffman didn't appear in these, not that Daniel immediately spotted anyway, but he could hardly bring himself to care. What did appear, were the faces of dozens of Hitler's young acolytes.

Gael leaned forward with a smirk. "Well? Is this what you're looking for?"

Daniel nodded slowly, his voice calm. "This is exactly what I need."

He carefully collected the photos, sliding them back into the folder as if they were nothing more than routine documents. But his mind raced—he was holding both more and less than what he'd come to find. This was evidence of a network, a whole group of young people tied to the growing Nazi movement in Argentina.

Gael's smug expression didn't falter, even as Daniel rose from his seat. "I assume this means you'll get me that interview?"

Daniel smiled tightly. "I'll do my best, Señor Fernandez. You've been very helpful."

As he turned to leave, Daniel couldn't resist asking one last question.

"Tell me, why haven't you printed any of these pictures before? Surely a paper like *El Sensacional* would love the scandal."

Gael waved a hand dismissively, his voice casual, almost flippant. "Nazism is terrible and all that, but these are just kids, you know? Young boys and girls who want to feel like they're part of something. No need to ruin their lives over it. It's harmless."

Daniel's jaw clenched at the word *harmless*. He felt any lingering sense of guilt evaporate in that instant. There was nothing harmless about what these young people were involved in, and Gael's ignorance—and his willingness to downplay it—made him seem not only obsequious, but dangerous.

With a nod, Daniel stepped out of the office clutching the manila folder tight in his hands. Every step he took toward the newsroom's exit was a step further away from the fetid atmosphere of gossip and celebrity worship that had infected the paper.

Outside, the fresh air hit him like a tonic. Daniel allowed himself a moment to breathe deeply, his mind already racing with the next steps. The photographic evidence was now in his possession, and with it, they could track down even more members of the new Nazi movement.

As Daniel walked back into the thrumming heart of the city, he couldn't help but think that Gael Fernandez would never know just how badly he'd been fooled. And Daniel, for one, felt no remorse about it.

~~~

Felipe adjusted his collar and wiped a thin sheen of sweat from his brow. Buenos Aires—with its dense traffic, the sound of Spanish mingling with the occasional English or German, and a humidity that clung to Felipe like an unwanted cloak—was vibrant and alive. Even in the cool, shadowed lobby of *The Herald*—the English-language paper where English Argentinians got their news—he could feel the heat of the city clinging to him.

The office was modest but retained the stateliness of British influence. Dark oak desks cluttered with papers, brass lamps with green glass shades, a portrait of Queen Elizabeth hanging behind the reception desk. At the desk, a stern woman in her fifties peered at Felipe over low-sitting glasses.

"You're here to see Mr. Taylor, correct?" the woman asked in sharp English with a clipped Buenos Aires accent.

"Yes, ma'am." Felipe gave her a tight smile. "Thomas Taylor. He's expecting me."

The receptionist's heels clicked against the tile floor as she led him down a narrow corridor lined with black-and-white photographs of past editors, dignitaries, and war correspondents. The scent of ink and paper brought on a wave of nostalgia Felipe didn't quite expect. He remembered walking into Daniel's office years ago—papers strewn everywhere, the scent of cigars mingling with books and newspapers from all over the world. Those memories felt like a lifetime ago.

The door at the end of the hall opened, and Thomas Taylor stepped out. He was tall, with sandy-brown hair, dressed sharply in a tailored gray suit that looked out of place in the otherwise chaotic newsroom. Taylor extended a hand as well as a polite but reserved smile.

"Mr. Montoya, was it?" Taylor asked, his voice refined and distinctly British.

"Indeed. Thank you for taking the time to meet with me," Felipe said as he shook Taylor's hand firmly.

They entered Taylor's office, which overlooked the bustling streets below. Felipe could see the edge of the Plaza de Mayo in the distance, its trees swaying in the hot breeze, the square dotted with people as cars trundled by. The walls of the office were lined with bookshelves filled with old volumes of newspapers, leather-bound books, and stacks of manila folders. The scent of old paper lingered in the air, mixing with the faint tang of fresh ink.

Taylor gestured for Felipe to sit in one of the worn leather chairs opposite his desk, which was meticulously organized, and a neat stack of papers and photographs were tucked into a small tray.

"So," Taylor began, sitting down and folding his hands on the desk. "You're from Scotland Yard, you said?"

Felipe nodded, careful to keep his expression neutral and his back straight, as Daniel had taught him. His was perhaps the biggest gamble of their three-part rouse.

"I'm with the Metropolitan Police Service, yes. Here on some, well, sensitive business."

Taylor raised an eyebrow, intrigued. "Sensitive?"

Felipe nodded gravely. "We've been investigating Nazi uprisings on college campuses here in Buenos Aires. We believe the son of a high-ranking Nazi propagandist is stirring up trouble, trying to recruit young men into extremist activities."

Taylor leaned back in his chair, eyes narrowing slightly. "Go on."

"We've received multiple tips about his involvement," Felipe continued, his voice taking on a tone of urgency, "but every time we try to confirm his presence at these events, we come up short. No photographs, no records of his participation. As if someone is protecting him."

Taylor raised an eyebrow. "And this is Scotland Yard's business because?"

Felipe gave a knowing smile and leaned forward just slightly.

"We have reason to believe that this boy harbors a particular grudge against English Argentinians. You see, during World War II, when most of Argentina remained neutral, many English Argentinians joined the British armed forces. This boy, as twisted as it may seem, views them as traitors, specifically targeting them because of their ties to Britain."

Taylor's face remained impassive, but Felipe could see the faintest flicker of concern in his eyes.

"And you believe this could escalate into something . . . larger?"

"We do," Felipe said solemnly. "We believe his hatred and rhetoric may lead to organized attacks, potentially in England as well. We've intercepted intel suggesting that this young man is trying to inspire anti-English sentiment within a broader Nazi network that still operates in shadows."

Taylor crossed his arms, the skepticism still lingering. "And this boy—his identity? You're certain he's here?"

Felipe paused for just a moment, as if weighing his next words carefully. "We believe he's the son of a British woman and a German man. His mother was turned against England by his father's influence, and this hatred has only grown since then. His father was one of Goebbels' inner circle members, a propagandist who knew how to stir hatred like few others."

Taylor uncrossed his arms, his expression softening. Felipe sensed he was close.

"This boy," Felipe added, his voice dropping to an almost conspiratorial whisper, "has a deep, personal vendetta. The reports suggest that his hatred stems from his twisted relationship with his mother—how she abandoned her English roots for her husband's ideology. The boy has become a puppet of his father's hatred—hatred that is now spilling out toward all of England."

Taylor let out a slow breath and leaned forward, elbows resting on the desk. "You mentioned something about photographs?"

Felipe nodded. "We believe there may be photographs of this boy from a recent protest at one of the universities. Some newspapers declined to publish these images. Perhaps due to legal threats."

Taylor stared at him for a long moment before standing abruptly.

"I may have something of interest to you," he said, walking over to the filing cabinet behind his desk. He pulled open a drawer with a heavy clunk and began flipping through folders until he found what he was looking for. He pulled out a thin folder and returned to his desk, opening it in front of Felipe.

Inside were several photographs, some faded, others still sharp with clarity. Felipe noticed an image of students gathered in front of the university's main building. Some held signs; others stood with arms crossed, their faces lost in shadow. Felipe's heart quickened when he saw a gangly figure on the edge of the group. The young man's face was partially turned away from the camera, but the profile was unmistakable.

It was Nils Hoffman.

Taylor tapped the photograph lightly with his finger. "This is from a protest just a few weeks ago. We were going to run the story, but . . ." he trailed off.

Felipe didn't let him finish. "Who stopped you?"

Taylor hesitated, glancing at the door as if someone might be listening.

"There were . . . legal threats. From a woman claiming to represent the interests of one of the students. She said the photo would compromise his safety."

"Lotte," Felipe murmured to himself. "Did she give a reason?"

"She gave every reason under the sun," Taylor said with a frown. "We didn't want to risk it. She was very insistent."

"I had the impression this wasn't her first time cleaning up after the boy, so to speak," he added cautiously. Felipe leaned back in his chair, his mind racing. He had the photograph now—proof of Nils's involvement. But this only confirmed what they feared, that Nils was part of something larger, and there were people willing to protect him at all costs.

Felipe stood, extending his hand once more. "Thank you for your cooperation, Mr. Taylor. This will be very helpful to our investigation."

Taylor shook his hand firmly. "If there's anything else, don't hesitate to ask."

Felipe gave a tight nod and turned to leave. As he stepped out into the heat of Buenos Aires once more, he allowed himself a brief moment of satisfaction. They were one step closer to uncovering the truth. But as he tucked the photograph into his coat pocket, he couldn't shake the feeling that they were running out of time.

CHAPTER TWELVE

The apartment building blueprints were sprawled across Giselle's kitchen table, the stark architectural lines hinting at the complex lives they concealed. Beneath the surface of ordinary apartments and functional communal spaces, Felipe knew that a hidden world existed—a lair of the past, its inhabitants bound together by a monstrous legacy.

From their vantage point, Giselle's cozy apartment felt infinitely removed from the sinister secrets lurking across the wide avenue. Elena—oblivious to the tension crackling in the air—scribbled happily in a coloring book, a cheerful soundtrack to their grim strategizing. Giselle's gaze lingered on her daughter, the innocence in her bright eyes a painful reminder of the forces threatening to shatter their fragile sense of security.

Their trifold effort to obtain incriminating evidence on Nils Hoffman had been a partial success, but it didn't give them a great deal to work with. They couldn't very well rush to police at this point—even if they managed to get the boy arrested, they would also send Adolf Hitler and any other higher-ups deeper into hiding. Aliases would be changed. Operatives would relocate. They would lose any progress they had made.

So, for now, they would keep the discoveries about Nils as an ace up their sleeve and move onto the next important piece of their investigation.

"Here," Felipe said, tracing a fingertip along the basement level of the plans. "The mail room. Direct access from the underground garage. It's our best chance . . . our only chance, really."

Daniel leaned in, his eyes narrowing in focus. "We need to know who lives there. Their names, connections—any scrap of information that could crack this wide open."

His voice echoed the determination they all felt. A flicker of hope finally pierced the gloom that had settled over their investigation.

The plan emerged quickly, shaped by a mix of desperation and necessity. The mail room was their key—a potential treasure trove of information. The task involved discreetly gaining entry into this secure facility without triggering any alerts. Over the next few days, they transformed the café across the street into their unofficial headquarters. From their window table, the trio observed the building's comings and goings with a meticulous focus on big-game players, while Elena busied herself drawing with crayons.

A consistent pattern emerged. The groundskeeper, an elderly man with a weathered face, swept the driveway each morning with clockwork precision. Around three o'clock, the mail carrier arrived, his worn leather satchel bulging with letters and packages. His gait was marked by a pronounced limp, probably a legacy of some long-forgotten injury.

The café patrons buzzed around them, oblivious to the silent drama unfolding across the street. Giselle, ever observant, noticed a change in Felipe. His usually stoic demeanor had softened slightly around the edges, a glimmer of his old self shining through. The proximity to their goal seemed to have reignited a spark within him; their plan, however risky, held the promise of resolution.

Daniel, ever the consummate strategist, mapped out their plan.

"The groundskeeper leaves around midday, opening a window of opportunity. The mail carrier . . . he's both our weakness and our way in." His eyes met Felipe's, a silent understanding passing between them.

The days stretched on forever in tense anticipation, a waiting game where each tick of the clock felt like the countdown to detonation. Buenos Aires swirled around them; a vibrant tapestry woven with the threads of ordinary lives. From their vantage point, they were both part of this chaotic symphony and entirely alien to it. Their world had narrowed to a singular focus: the apartment building, the mailroom, and the desperate hope that within those unremarkable walls, the truth they craved was waiting.

~~~

The mid-afternoon sun cast long shadows across the bustling street as Felipe stepped out of the café, heart pounding in his chest. This was it. The moment their desperate plan hinged upon, a gamble that could either ignite their investigation or send it crashing into failure. Across the way, the apartment building loomed, silent and deceptively innocuous.

The mail carrier emerged from the side alley, his limp pronounced as he hefted the worn satchel onto his shoulder. Felipe took a steadying breath and crossed the street, his steps calculated and purposeful.

"Señor," he called out as he approached, a touch of urgency in his voice. "May I have a word?"

The mailman turned, surprise registering on his lined face. His faded blue eyes etched with weariness met Felipe's with a flicker of suspicion. Up close, Felipe noted the name embroidered on his uniform pocket: Joaquin. A wave of hope washed over him; a name was a thread, a piece of the tangible reality they sought amidst the shadows.

"I see your limp has been giving you trouble," Felipe said, gesturing towards Joaquin's uneven gait. "I know someone, a specialist, who could help with that." He hesitated, gauging the mail carrier's reaction.

Joaquin's eyes narrowed.

"What do you mean, 'help'?"

His voice was rough, laced with the wariness of a man who had walked the hard streets of Buenos Aires for too many years.

With a calculated gesture, Felipe produced an envelope from his pocket and pressed it into Joaquin's callused hand. He felt the man's body stiffen, his curiosity warring with caution.

"This might make it easier to see this specialist," Felipe said, his voice low.

Joaquin's fingers fumbled with the envelope, a frown furrowing his brow as he pulled out the contents. His eyes widened in shock, his mouth forming a silent 'o' as he stared down at the stack of neatly trimmed hundred-dollar bills. Except, they weren't whole. Each bill had been meticulously cut in half, rendered useless in their current form.

"What kind of game is this?" Joaquin's voice rose, the accusation hanging heavy in the air. "You think you can mock me with these . . . these scraps of paper?"

Felipe held his ground and locked eyes with Joaquin.

"Consider it a down payment, señor. The rest comes once you've helped me with a small matter."

"And what might that 'small matter' be?" Joaquin's voice held a dangerous edge now. He knew enough to understand the implications of half-paid bribes and mysterious strangers.

Felipe leaned in closer, lowering his voice to a near whisper.

"Information, señor. Nothing too difficult. Surely a man in your position knows a thing or two about the residents who receive your deliveries."

Joaquin flinched slightly, a muscle twitching in his weathered cheek.

"You're talking about tampering with the mail, sí? You want me to violate my oath . . . that's a crime, señor." His voice had dropped to a hiss, laced with a mixture of fear and defiance.

"An oath to whom?" Felipe countered; his own voice tinged with quiet menace. "A faceless company, a government unconcerned with the struggles of ordinary men?"

He saw the flicker of hesitation in Joaquin's eyes, the battle waging within the man. There was pride in those tired eyes, a stubborn adherence to duty. But there was also the desperation of someone who had known too many hard days.

"The money," Joaquin began, his voice strained. "If I were to help you . . . there would be serious consequences if anyone found out."

Felipe delivered the final blow, his voice a promise rich with temptation. "One thousand more, in whole bills, señor. That kind of money . . . it could change your life. Ease your burdens, perhaps help with that leg of yours."

He watched as Joaquin wavered, the lure of financial security battling his ingrained sense of right and wrong. This man held the key to unlocking their tightly guarded fortress, but at what cost? Felipe felt a strange pang of guilt knowing he was exploiting the very system that kept this ordinary man trapped.

The decision hung in the air; a silent battle waged in the tired eyes of a mail carrier on a Buenos Aires street. The future of their investigation, the desperate search for the monstrous ghosts haunting their lives—rested on the choice made by this unassuming man with a worn satchel and a limp that told its own story of hardship.

~~~

The remains of their dinner—a traditional Argentinian asado with vibrant chimichurri sauce—sat half-heartedly cleared to the side of the kitchen counter. The tantalizing scent of grilled meat lingered in the air, a stark contrast to the tension that had settled over the room. Laughter drifted in from the living room where Elena and Charlene, oblivious to the adults' anxieties, were engaged in a spirited make-believe tea party.

Giselle carefully lifted a piece of mail with a paper towel, her touch delicate, almost reverent. It was as if the mundane envelopes held the weight of history itself. With practiced care, they sorted the stack, their movements a silent choreography born of necessity. Felipe's voice broke the tense silence.

"That was a smart move, Giselle. Cutting the bills like that . . . " he trailed off, his admiration laced with a twinge of guilt.

Giselle nodded grimly. "Desperate times . . ." she murmured. Lying to Karen—the woman who'd become a friend, the woman who was now excitedly planning her wedding—was unbearable. The deceit gnawed at her, a constant reminder of the impossible balancing act they were engaged in. Her gaze lingered on Charlene, so innocent, so trusting, and a sharp pang hit her. Weren't they all children once? Innocent of the cruel divisions the adult world would impose upon them? But then came the choices, the compromises, and the blurred lines no amount of naive wishing could erase.

Daniel, sensing her turmoil, offered a reassuring smile.

"Think of it this way, Giselle. Having Charlene here shows Karen we're still in her corner. Keeps up appearances."

Felipe echoed the sentiment, his voice softening. "And soon, mi amor, soon this will all be over. We'll find what we came for, and we'll have our lives back."

His eyes met hers, their shared longing for a balm against the relentless pressure. It was a promise, a flickering hope in a world of shadows and doubt.

The pile of unopened mail lay before them, each innocent-looking envelope potentially concealing a devastating truth. With a deep breath, Giselle began methodically listing the residents, meticulously recording each distinctly German name. "Twelve apartments . . . " she said, the starkness of the number hanging in the air.

Three single women. Five single men. Four couples. The pieces refused to form a coherent picture. Who were these people? Conspirators, pawns, or simply those whose family ties damned them by association?

"Lotte Braun," Felipe said, tracing the familiar name on an envelope. "Apartment 502. Not the penthouse as we assumed." A flicker of disappointment crossed his face. They had built an elaborate mental hierarchy, placing the highest-ranking conspirators at the very top. This piece of information felt like a misstep, a blow to their carefully constructed theories.

The name Romilda Lehmann in elegant script stared up at them from the penthouse apartment's return address. Intrigue flared, quickly followed by a sense of foreboding.

"Who is she?" Giselle murmured, dread settling in her stomach.

The Tel Aviv postmark on one of Romilda Lehmann's envelopes commanded their attention. Israel. The relentless hunters of those who had escaped justice. It felt both encouraging—knowing there were forces actively working against the Nazi remnants—and deeply unsettling to see the tangible connection laid bare. Next, Damascus. A chilling reminder that evil had no single address, that it wove its insidious tendrils across the globe.

Their sense of triumph from successfully accessing the building's mail had vanished and was replaced by an overwhelming tide of new questions. Romilda Lehmann, her penthouse, and mail coming from within Israel . . . It was as if with each answer, a multitude of new mysteries unraveled before them.

Felipe broke the heavy silence, his voice a mixture of weariness and determination.

"Back to Joaquin tomorrow. We'll replace these items, keep him in our corner."

Daniel carefully read the letter from Tel Aviv aloud, translating each cryptic sentence into a chilling reality.

"*My Dear Romilda,*" he began, his voice low and measured. "*I am soon to end my visit to this damned country, the—hopefully temporary—residence of our dear friend.*" He paused, his eyes flicking to Giselle and then back to the letter.

"*He came here, as you know, for medical treatment—prostate . . . not surprising at his age.*"

A collective gasp escaped their lips. The room seemed to shrink, the air thick with a suffocating silence.

"*He did not want to have the surgery here,*" Daniel continued, "*although he knew the doctors and hospitals there are first class. He just did not want to run the risk of talking too loosely on account of the anesthetics and medications he would be given.*

Given that he lives like a recluse and rarely leaves his home, his spirits are remarkably good. He misses you and the boy . . . but accepts that is how it is. You would not recognize him. Thank God for the surgery, our friends in Rome and Zurich, and all the steps he has taken with their help.

I cannot tell you how grateful I will be to leave this place again. I've visited him to express my appreciation to him, but I am equally appreciative that I can say I'm dropping this off at the post on my way out of this bedeviled country—hopefully for good.

I hope you are well. I think of you always.

Greetings, Klaus."

". . . he lives like a recluse," Giselle repeated. She seemed to examine each of the phrases from the letter that drifted out of her, trying to make something of their condensed and summarized forms.

". . . thank god for the surgery . . . you would not recognize him."

Felipe's voice was barely a whisper.

"Hitler."

Their eyes met across the table, with the significance of the name becoming evident to both parties. Had their relentless pursuit truly led them to the architect of monstrous evil? Was the face of their enemy now hidden in plain sight, forever altered by the desperate measures of a cornered fugitive? And the mysterious Klaus, his cryptic message filled with an unsettling familiarity . . . another ghost, another name to add to their ever-growing list.

Giselle shivered, a wave of nausea washing over her. Their triumphant breakthrough now felt like a descent into a far deeper labyrinth. The pieces scattered before them refused to coalesce—instead, multiplying, twisting, and taunting them with their incompleteness. It was a chilling reminder that finding Hitler, proving his continued existence, would not bring closure. The evil he represented had poisoned generations, its insidious tendrils weaving through lives they would never fully comprehend. Theirs was a battle against shadows, a desperate chase for a truth that threatened to consume them entirely.

CHAPTER THIRTEEN

olonel Judd's voice crackled over the international line, a familiar rasp cutting through the humid Buenos Aires air.

"Daniel, we've got a partial match on the fingerprint from the champagne flute."

Right to it this time, Daniel thought. No talk about radishes, kale, or natural pesticides. The worn leather of his chair creaked beneath him as he assumed the posture of a solider whose commanding officer had just made eye contact.

"Partial?"

"About seventy-five percent certainty. Not enough to act on, but enough to know we're on the right track. And that's something—"

Daniel felt he got better over the years at reigning in emotions that were clearly unhelpful to situation, reactions others might have termed "outbursts"—but some situations were bound to tap into his more primitive self.

"It's more than something!" he roared. "It's *great*. This means—"

"Daniel."

Taking his own turn to interrupt, Judd—in a tone more resolute than he ever used when talking about soil moisture content—said, "We need one-hundred-percent here. You know that as well as I do. I know how eager you are to move forward with this. But you know damn well how badly it will go if you accuse the wrong person of gallivanting around with

Adolf Hitler—if it comes to light all you had to go on was a seventy-five percent match to a fingerprint."

Daniel did know. He knew it would devastate their cause, their chance of ever being able to track him down again. Not to mention what it would do for Daniel's personal reputation. At the same time, a good reputation would mean nothing more to him than some airport gift shop trinket if he knew in his own mind, heart, and acidic gut that he'd let any member of the Nazi aristocracy escape.

Judd couldn't see Daniel nodding, but he could assume his assent from the silence.

"Do you see another chance coming up to collect prints?" Judd asked.

Daniel leaned back in his chair, causing it to groan from an entirely different sort of ache. This was where things got interesting. He proceeded to tell Judd about Karen's upcoming wedding, the opportunity for unfettered access to Lotte, Nils, and a particularly important figure.

"We think there's a possibility we may actually see Eva herself," Daniel said.

"Eva Braun," he clarified.

The colonel remained quiet for a couple seconds before asking, in a voice soft with disbelief, why Daniel would ever imagine such a thing was possible.

Judd's tone didn't seem to accuse Daniel of fabricating a breakthrough nor interrogate his sanity. For a moment, Daniel wasn't sure what it was in Judd's voice that unnerved him so. Whatever it was, he was rattled enough that it took him a beat to produce all the logical reasons for assuming Eva may attend.

He shared how Karen had told Giselle she would elope with Hans in the middle of the night and be done with it, but she knew her family would never forgive her. How Karen had specifically mentioned an aunt who loved weddings—her own had apparently wound up some rushed, clandestine af-fair—and how sure Karen was that this same aunt would show up expecting pageantry and grandeur.

"And you think the aunt has to be Eva Braun," Judd supplied.

Both men were privy enough to the Nazi social gears to know that Eva had (finally) wed Hitler only as the Allies were closing in on the two of them. It was known to anyone who kept up with such things that Eva had been the one to pursue Hitler, evaluating him as some outsider prince within a fairytale version of Deutschland. Hers was the sort of admiration destined to thaw his frosty ego, and one day it finally did. One day, he went from thinking of her as an attractive little thing—if far too boisterous for a woman—to thinking of her as his wife.

It's unlikely that her fantasies of their wedding day were staged in a bunker with Hitler scared for his miserable life. It was meant to be her crowning day—not something that could be interpreted by outsiders, to her great humiliation, as an act of deathbed desperation.

And then they hadn't died after all. They had survived, only to be immediately forced into the fringes and shadows. Nev-er again showing their real faces, holding hands in public, or revealing their actual names to strangers. How often had she probably preoccupied herself with idle daydreams of shaking a good German's hand and introducing herself as Eva Hitler?

Of course she would show up, brimming with maternal-adjacent party planning vigor for her niece's wedding to a Good German Man. Once Daniel started thinking about it in detail and forming the logic into words, he was able to easily articulate this cornerstone of his theory about Eva showing her face.

But still.

Judd was right to be skeptical. The idea that Eva Braun would risk exposure to sign autographs as "Frau Hitler" was absurd—she belonged in the shadows with her husband, like cockroaches in a dark corner, avoiding light and the thud of footsteps.

What Daniel couldn't quite figure out was why it bothered him that Judd had received this information with healthy mistrust. Daniel had looked at it how he looked at every other detail of this case.

Up until now, he, Felipe, and Giselle had focused on their incredible luck:

Karen's habit of writing her birth surname in full. When she started the scribble of what looked like an *e* to Felipe, it cracked open an investigative file on Charlene's doe-eyed nanny. Lotte getting plastered at her birthday party and regaling mixed company with a story whose facts were so minimally changed that the team could use it confidently to match Lotte to Gretl Braun. Nils changing his real last name by only a single letter, as though to say, "Eh, good enough."

And that, Daniel realized, was the rub.

He, Felipe, and Giselle had attributed their successes to the carelessness of their targets: a group of Nazis who evaded justice for so long that they had accidentally grown complacent—lucky for everyone trying to stop them.

In response to Giselle coming home from Lotte's fifty-second birthday party with a purse full of evidence the partygoers had been too drunk or preoccupied to miss—and in response to every other "break" in the mystery—they had been somewhat blinded by their own elation.

All they had been able to see was this: they were closing in on Hitler.

They were *winning*.

Felipe was edging ever closer to his dream of making the world a safer place for his daughter, and in the process salving scars he had accumulated back in Paraguay.

Daniel was finishing what he'd started long ago. Avenging his own sons. Making a strike for the unlikely team of himself and his ex-wife, Claudia. Guiding his niece and Felipe, his protégé and friend, into a happier life.

That's what they all focused on when the carelessness of Hitler's followers came into view—how it enabled the three of them to right the wrongs—internationally, yes—but also within the deep, private recesses of their personal lives.

But now, talking to Judd, Daniel saw it differently. Lotte, Nils, and even Karen's carelessness wasn't a mere byproduct of complacency; they were living in accordance with how they looked at themselves. Untouchable. This was the crowd that escaped a worldwide manhunt and made a comfortable, even luxurious, home for themselves in broad daylight.

Everything they'd been through had only further convinced them of their unassailability, and therefore the righteousness of their dreadful "cause." There was only a single instance he could think of when the bastards seemed firmly on the defensive, and that had only been about keeping Nils's picture out of the paper.

Daniel's pulse drummed in his neck like a ticking bomb.

"I'm coming down to Buenos Aires." Judd's voice broke through his thoughts. "I'll be on standby for the wedding to ensure no evidence gets lost or corrupted."

Daniel appreciated Judd's dedication; it was something he could always count on, but now he was thinking anew about all the support they would need if they were to pull this off. The target crowd may be criminally smug, but that alone didn't make them sitting ducks. They had their reasons for feeling inviolable. And one of those reasons—their security detail—was likely to be swarming Karen's wedding with guns tucked inside their three-button, high-gorge, slim-fitting suit jackets.

"What about the CIA?" Daniel asked. "The Pentagon? I appreciate the hell for you coming here, Judd, but we're going to need everybody we can get on this."

With a deep sigh that accounted for both what he was about to say and the reaction he anticipated from Daniel, Judd said, "You know the Eichmann debacle has made things . . . complicated."

Judd was referring to a man by the name of Otto Adolf Eichmann, a Nazi higher-up as well as a chief organizer of the Holocaust. When he was captured and detained by the Allies in 1945, the world celebrated too soon, and the despicable worm had escaped to Argentina. There he successfully hid—as too many Nazi escapees would—until Mossad tracked him down in Buenos Aires in 1960. Put on trial before the Supreme Court of Israel and convicted in Jerusalem, he had been executed in 1962—a mere two years ago.

In Argentina, Eichmann's capture had been met with far-right anti-Semitic demonstrations, to put it mildly. In a time that should have, in Daniel's opinion, been focused on celebrating the toppling of another Nazi orchestrator, he'd been forced to listen to a symphony of concerns over Argentina's sovereignty.

Then there were all the rumblings to the effect that maybe, just maybe, the CIA had been aware of Eichmann's whereabouts for some time but kept the information from Israel to protect the United States's interests vis-à-vis the Cold War.

It wasn't that Daniel exactly needed Judd to dust off the Eichmann file; he'd been paying attention to it all along. He knew the facts backward. But it was also true that he'd been able to convince himself that if the world ever had a viable shot at capturing Hitler again, the tenuous, convoluted webs of international diplomacy would bend or break—or whatever the hell needed to happen for a monster to find his lasting prison.

"The U.S. government is wary of getting involved at a federal level," Judd said, suddenly sounding as tired as Daniel had ever heard. "And the local authorities are . . . well, let's just say we can't trust the Buenos Aires police. Some of them may have been complicit in hiding Nazis, and those who weren't are still bitter about what they see as a trampling of their authority."

To Daniel, this was a perfect example of what he had merely thought about Hitler's Argentinian cohorts: they were cocky bastards—for solid reasons. Inhumane, wrong, and foolish reasons, but solid ones. Governmental forces morally bound to hunt them down were wringing their hands over the thought of losing ground in the Cold War but not stepping on the toes or pride of local authorities . . . would they really shirk their duty of stopping the world's most notorious mass murder for these justifications?

Daniel slammed his fist on the desk, the sound echoing against the walls of Giselle and Felipe's kitchen, where he sat at their round table talking to Judd.

"So we're on our own?" he roared. For a split second, it occurred to him that he was being loud enough to wake Elena if she was asleep—if she was even here right now. They seemed to be living in a blur where days and hours fused together. Despite his best efforts, he couldn't remember if it was a Saturday and the little girl was sleeping in, if she was off shopping with her mother, or if she was playing with a friend.

To be safe, Daniel lowered his voice. "Just the four of us?"

"Not quite," Judd replied. "I have a few favors I can call in. Some old Marine buddies who owe me their lives. They'll be discreet, but effective."

Daniel felt a flicker of hope. It wasn't much, but it was something. They weren't alone in this fight. With renewed determination, he said, "Alright, Judd. Let's bring these bastards to justice."

The line went silent for a moment before Judd's voice came back, steady and unwavering.

"Damn right we will."

~~~

The day after his phone call with Daniel, Judd arrived in Buenos Aires. The group wasted no time in showing him the letter to Romilda Lehmann, the enigmatic woman who resided in the penthouse of Lotte's apartment building. Judd read the letter with a skeptical eye, noting Klaus's reference to their "dear friend" in Israel, a phrase that had sent shivers down his spine, as it had done to each of his colleagues.

It's the word "friend," he thought. *It's so soft. So . . . human.*

"This is potentially huge," Judd admitted, "but we have to be careful. We don't even know who Romilda Lehmann is, much less who this 'dear friend' of hers might be."

"But you know she's important!" Felipe cried. His eyes sparkled with a sort of hypomania this morning, the kind a young man got from lying awake half the night thinking, *Tomorrow Judd gets here, and then our plan* really *gets underway.*

"What I know is that some assumptions are being made here," Judd said.

Giselle tipped her chair back with a heavily sleeping Elena in her arms. Her eyes roamed from Judd, looking both wary and weary, to Felipe—whom she wanted to encourage join Elena in taking a nap—to her uncle Daniel. He appeared lost in the thought, which he had more or less continued since his conversation with Judd the previous day.

"But, Colonel Judd," Giselle countered, "the implications are clear. The letter *strongly* suggests that Hitler and Eva Braun are in Israel. This could be the biggest discovery of our lives."

Judd sighed. "I understand your excitement," he said. "I'm just worried we're getting ahead of ourselves."

Felipe leaned forward, his eyes swimming and on fire all at once.

"We've been careful, Judd. We've almost been more careful than I can stand!" He wasn't genuinely shouting. He was engaging in the fine art of speaking strenuously—ardently—but at a volume barely above a whisper, which he'd mastered in the years since Elena had been able to make out words.

The four adults barely fit around Giselle and Felipe's table. Lucky for them, Elena had been content to sleep on her mother's chest, the girl's cherubic, juice-stained face resting comfortably on Giselle's left shoulder. When Daniel drifted off in thought, he watched Elena. Watched her bird-like shoulders rise and fall with her delicate waves of breath. Watched the loose chocolate-covered curl dangling in front of her mouth shift with every gentle snore.

He seemed to snap out of it, though, when Judd said, "I'm an old man now"—and not only because he wasn't accustomed to hearing the colonel use the *o* word. Daniel's gaze—somehow languid despite being fueled by an unsettling mix of too much coffee with too little cream and too much bourbon with not enough ice—shifted to his mentor. *Old.* He didn't like hearing it any more than he could imagine Judd liked saying it.

And why was Judd saying it? Was this some sort of death-bed "imparting-of-wisdom" moment he'd flown across the Atlantic to deliver?

Daniel sat upright, feeling his brows sink low over his eyes.

"But I'm the only one in here who can say that."

Judd let the words sit there for a moment. Then he motioned with his chin—which was developing a snowy shadow from his failure to shave for the past day and a half—toward Elena or Giselle, or maybe both. By any account, it was Felipe he was addressing when he said, "A young man has more he's got to account for, and for longer."

Felipe's face betrayed a note of hurt as he said, "You don't think I know that? Giselle, Elena—they are my motivation for this, Colonel."

"And they'll be your motivation for life, son."

Son, Daniel repeated in his mind. Judd was bringing out the big guns.

"Where do you imagine you'll leave yourself . . . what do you think you'll be able to do for them five, ten years down the road if you ruin your reputation and your good name? If you burn through all your credit with people claiming you've found Adolf Hitler and come to find out all you've really found is a German family settled in Argentina, acting no more cagey than any other German family settled in Argentina?"

His words hung in the air like a criminal sentence being read aloud in court. And like the wife of a man convicted, Giselle opened her mouth and started to rise in protest. Daniel's hand on her shoulder seemed to bring her back into the scene that contained them all.

Then Daniel spoke up, for what seemed like the first time in hours. "No more *cagey*, Judd? What sort of harmless German family lives in a heavily-guarded apartment building that won't let strangers anywhere near them?"

"A rich one," Judd answered in a tone so plateaued that his words sounded relentlessly sensible. "A family guilty by association. One that came here because Germany was an unparalleled mess. Maybe they had nothing to do with the rise of Nazism. Maybe they turned a blind eye to it the way people do sometimes when life is happening on every side of them. And maybe they were criminally simplistic about how they voted come election time."

Maybe it was the exhaustion of enduring countless nights filled with burnt, cold coffee and strategy notes scrawled on blueprints, the backs of envelopes, and a spare school notebook they "borrowed" from Elena. By any account, Felipe didn't feel he could listen to this much longer. He could barely sit still.

"A person who didn't know you would think you're defending people who put Hitler in power," he said.

The sharp "He's not" that followed came from Daniel, as did a sideways glance meant to sober Felipe to the present moment, including the present company.

When Felipe sought eye contact with Giselle—wanting a sign that someone heard what he was hearing, that she felt the threat of their hard-won momentum being thwarted the way he did—he was surprised to find her gentle nod in agreement with Daniel, and with Colonel Judd.

And Judd was speaking again.

"What I'm saying is that they could be anywhere from perfectly innocent to guilty of things that would earn them a hell of a lot of contempt from good company." He leaned in for this one. "What I'm saying is that it's possible to imagine a family with some resources that falls anywhere along that spectrum of culpability fleeing Germany to somewhere that's been only too welcoming . . . but also noticing the unrest in the air about stuff like what Daniel and I were talking about—stuff like Eichmann. Seeing that it's possible for the guilty to be hunted down far from their own backyard and executed in Israel—and knowing good and well that sometimes people take things too far: mobs rule and the innocent, or at least less guilty, get a mighty suspicious eye cast on them."

Judd looked pointedly at Daniel.

"Might make for a bit of caginess, don't you think?"

Daniel didn't say a word, he only returned the colonel's long, flat gaze. Felipe, on the other hand, had every intention of forming words—likely a torrent of them—but before he could speak, Giselle did.

"And think if we're wrong. It's hard enough to imagine looking somebody in the eye who might not have had anything to do with it and point-blank asking—"

To everyone sitting around the table watching her, it looked as though Giselle suddenly let out her frustration with the impossibility of her situation. She let her words hang in the air.

"Of course," Judd conceded. "I'm not talking about letting the lead go cold. What I am talking about is proceeding with all the caution we can afford."

The day passed in a flurry of research as the four of them— a group often reduced to three when one of them would depart to play with Elena—searched for information about Romilda Lehmann, the identity of Klaus, and what contacts in Israel might help uncover who Romilda's "dear friend" was.

In every case, they came up empty. Romilda Lehmann appeared nowhere outside of the typical search results—archival birth, marriage, and death records, each and every one of which they had traced to an empty end. One person named Romilda had been deceased eleven years now. Another would have been six years old and living in London with her family. Felipe was excited that their search found no record of a living Romilda Lehmann matching the age range of their Romilda Lehmann theory. Judd had been quick to shake his head, gently but firmly.

"All we are missing is access to one birth or marriage certificate. And God knows what records got destroyed in the fight."

"Or," Giselle posited, "it could be like Judd said. Maybe this is someone who's going by a name that gives her some privacy. Maybe even because she doesn't want past voting records or associations getting out . . ."

She would neither finish her statement nor look her husband in the eye.

"And who are we thinking she even is?" Judd asked. "If you've got reason to believe that Eva is with Hitler, and Hitler's in Israel—"

"And Gretl Braun is accounted for," Daniel supplied, his eyes glazed over in thought.

"Then what high-ranking female figure in the Nazi party does that even leave room for this Romilda to be?" Judd finished.

To that, Felipe had no answer, no rebuttal. His eyes glazed over as he tried to contend with the numerous dead-ends they had for Klauses who could be intimately or tangentially connected to Hitler.

He crossed the room to get himself a drink before heading upstairs.

While Giselle and Felipe tucked Elena into bed, Judd rifled through the boxes of pasta, sauce jars, and refrigerator crispers until he'd acquired enough to whip them up a vegetable lasagna. As the bleary-eyed crew dug in, Judd mentioned—in the voice of a man with one foot already in his dreams—that this was his wife's favorite. That if they'd been at his place in Connecticut, everything short of noodles could've been made from scratch.

Felipe took longer than necessary chewing, as though his jaw muscles were as spent as his mind.

"Daniel," he finally said, "what about your contacts in Israel? Who are we going to be able to count on to help us get information when we go?"

His voice said it all. He didn't really care that they hadn't found candidates for the real Romilda Lehmann or Klaus, nor that evidence suggested they didn't exist. The fact that Klaus was such a common German name didn't deteriorate his motivation. Even if his own wife was growing weary of this hunt, and possibly of his blind enthusiasm for it . . . well, he'd just have to keep in mind that she was one of the biggest reasons he was doing this.

Daniel knew Felipe well enough now to read all of that and more in his question. In the same vein, he knew that not even the next bit of news he had to share would dissuade Felipe from doing what he felt he must—with the vigor and will of a Secret Service agent throwing himself between a bullet and a U.S. President. So he just said it.

"There's no one, Felipe. I've always got an in with Mossad—we can walk through those doors and put a bug in their ears anytime. But not until we have something to come to them with. The director they've got in there now is no fan of mine."

This was true. The current director had inherited the obligation to take a meeting with Daniel Lavy upon taking the job, but he was one of many agents who looked at Daniel as the sort of man who—being too rogue even for Mossad—could only be counted on to make things unpredictable and messy.

"So what you're saying . . ." Felipe began.

"Is that we can go," Daniel filled in without hesitation. "We should go. But until we've scoped out Hitler ourselves, we shouldn't count on help. For that part, it's just us."

CHAPTER FOURTEEN

The Aerolíneas Argentinas jet sliced through the clouds—a silver streak against the cerulean sky. Inside the cabin, the air hummed with the low thrum of engines punctuated by the clinking of silverware against china as the flight attendants served dinner. The aroma of roasted chicken and garlic wafted through the air, mingling with the faint scent of leather from the seats. Had this been the first step of some exotic vacation on which they were embarking, it would have boded well.

Felipe leaned back in his seat, gaze fixed on the wispy clouds outside the window. The roar of engines seemed to amplify the thoughts swirling in his mind. Beside him, Daniel stirred even as his eyes remained closed.

Here was the thing about Daniel: he always seemed to know when Felipe needed him, eyes closed or not.

"You're going over the plan again and again and again, aren't you?" he mumbled.

Felipe nodded, entirely certain Daniel could sense him doing so.

"Hard not to. We pull this off, we change history."

Now Daniel opened his eyes, but he didn't turn his gaze on Felipe. Perhaps he was still in that hazy but heightened headspace between sleep and wakefulness. Perhaps it was that he'd been quietly contemplating—with absolutely no purposeful effort—Judd's turn as a paternal, cautious, nearly finger-wagging figure to him since their phone call before Judd's arrival in Buenos Aires.

Whatever was responsible for it, his reply to his younger comrade was this: "I realize what we're doing is delicate."

"I know," Felipe said in a voice of some protest. "And we're treating it delicately—wouldn't you say?"

In his eyes, they were exercising an abundance of caution to the mission with the double-pronged approach they had landed on: Judd and his brigade of retired Marine buddies stay behind to handle the wedding with Giselle, Daniel and himself coordinate with Mossad in Israel.

Although Daniel nodded, Felipe couldn't help but pick up on the slight reservation in his eyes as he said, "Yes . . . it's the best way to make sure we don't miss anything."

Felipe took a sip of the chilled beer the airline served in frosted mugs.

"Of course, of course. But you know it's more than just that." When the older man didn't take the bait, Felipe rushed on, "It's a way to potentially capture them *all*, Daniel. Every. Last. One of them."

As he was listing the names that compromised that ignoble list—Lotte and Nils obviously, but also Eva, Hitler, their security detail, maybe even Heinrich Hoffmann? Was it possible he would show up to snap a few award-winning pictures at the wedding, where his son would be dressed in Argentina's finest polished-gray cotton?

The two men fell silent, each lost in his own thoughts. The flight attendants cleared the dinner trays, and the cabin lights dimmed, casting the interior in a soft amber glow. The murmur of conversation from the other passengers faded into the background, replaced by the gentle lullaby of the engines.

Felipe closed his eyes, envisioning the scene that would unfold in Tel Aviv. Mossad agents—clad in dark suits and armed with the latest surveillance equipment—would surround the apartment building they believed Hitler to be living in. They would move with precision, their every move carefully choreographed.

For his part, Daniel was picturing a scene much less organized. Between his heavy blinks strobed a mental scene of the chaos that would erupt at the wedding when Judd and Giselle made their move. It would take only seconds for the guests to register in their nerve endings if not their conscious thoughts, that their high-brow social occasion was actually a cage. They'd try to escape—as animals do when they suddenly realize they're boxed in—before they've accepted it as the new way of things.

Animals—it's how they would act.

The proverbial claws would come out. The fangs. The venom.

They would do anything to escape.

And while it was true that Judd and several of his war-hardened retired Marine buddies would be on hand, until the moment the operation closed in on the wedding, there would be a single member of the team alone in the cage with the beasts.

Giselle.

CHAPTER FIFTEEN

The Tel Aviv sun beat down on the dusty streets as Felipe and Daniel emerged from the small rental office, clutching the keys to their rented Ford Zephyr. A balding, middle-aged man named Moshe, their designated driver, waited beside the vehicle with a cigarette dangling from his lips.

"Shalom," Moshe greeted them, letting the cigarette tumble from his mouth to the ground, where he crushed it without a glance.

"Ready to see the sights of Tel Aviv, gentlemen?"

Felipe uncrumpled the map that had resided in his pants pocket since he'd kissed his girls goodbye.

"Actually, we're looking for a specific location. It's a bit off the beaten path."

Daniel gestured for Moshe to examine a spot on the map.

"A friend of ours recommended a particular apartment building we'd like to check out. The main thing either of us can remember is that he said it's in an industrial area. We're thinking possibly around here."

With his index finger, Daniel drew an invisible circle around a neighborhood he and Felipe had decided was the likeliest candidate for serving as Adolf Hitler's hiding spot in Israel.

Moshe squinted at the map, then shrugged.

"Could be anywhere. This city doesn't have only one industrial zone."

Daniel wasn't surprised to hear this. A city as expansive as Tel Aviv would naturally be encircled by any number of production zones. However, this one bore careful consideration. For one thing, their city map of Tel Aviv showed a compact apartment complex sandwiched between a power plant on one side and a slew of warehouses on the other.

Their rented Ford sliced through the twisting streets of Tel Aviv, its tires humming a steady rhythm on the sunbaked asphalt. Moshe, their driver and tour guide of sorts, navigated the chaotic traffic with the ease of someone who had come of age driving these streets. His face represented a mosaic of ages—the excitable eyes of a young man glittered out from skin turned a leathery tan from countless hours under the Mediterranean sun. Smoker's lines deeply framed a mouth that seemed perpetually molded into a shape Felipe could only think of as "amused."

Daniel and Felipe—seated together in the backseat—stared out the window, their eyes scanning the passing cityscape. The air inside the car was heavy with anticipation, a combination of the men's profound sweat, and a cologne emanating from Moshe that smelled like a mix of coconut and bourbon. Daniel generally considered his stomach made of steel, but at the moment, he felt like their next stop at a red light might be his chance to lean out of the car and vomit his pita-and-hummus breakfast all over the road.

"So, this friend of yours," Moshe said, his voice gruff but not unkind, "he didn't give you anything except that this building is in some industrial zone?"

"No," Felipe replied, "the description was vague. Unfortunately, we'll just have to hope we know it when we spot it."

Moshe chuckled dryly.

"So, you're hoping to 'just know' the right building when you've never seen it before?" He swerved to avoid a scooter weaving through traffic, his features never betraying a flinch, and his hands continuing to glide over the steering wheel like water.

Yeah, Felipe thought dejectedly. *That's about the size of it.*

Moshe navigated the narrow alleyways, dodging pedestrians and street vendors with ease. The city was a vibrant tapestry of sights and sounds, a mix of old and new, East and West. Bauhaus-style buildings, all clean lines and white facades, stood alongside traditional Middle Eastern structures with their intricate mosaics and arched doorways.

As they ventured further from the city center, the landscape changed. The bustling streets gave way to industrial zones, dotted with warehouses and factories. The air grew heavy with the smell of oil and metal.

"Any of these look like 'the one'?" Moshe asked after somewhere between five and fifteen minutes had passed—this was the sort of sleepy heat that made time hard to keep track of. Felipe and Daniel blinked heavily as though awakening from deep sleep. Moshe was gesturing toward a row of nondescript warehouses that sat some five hundred feet from a squat, yellow apartment building.

Daniel narrowed his eyes at the building. Apart from his gut saying "no"—normally enough for him to act on, no further questions—there were specifics Daniel could put his finger on that disqualified this place as Hitler's home away from home. Namely, the patios were strewn with toys and brightly colored children's outfits hanging out to dry. This was a family residence through and through—the sort that would attract multigenerational visitors, schoolmates. Young parents becoming friends, sipping together on the patches of grass that stretched in front of ground-level apartments as they set up miniature playgrounds for children. Those children's shrieks of outdoor joy rising up and being absorbed by the walls of every apartment in the building.

Hitler, Daniel thought, *would blow his brains out. Which would make our job a hell of a lot easier.*

They had already visited half a dozen industrial zones, each one blending into the next in a monotonous blur of concrete and steel. Each nearby housing units struck Daniel and Felipe as somehow unfit for Hitler.

When his guests shook their heads at this building too, Moshe proposed a different sort of stop.

"It is lunchtime for me, gentlemen," he said. "I invite you to join me. There's a café not two minutes from here that serves a baba ghanoush that is simply"—he pressed his pinched fingers to his lips and released a dramatic air kiss. "After a bite to eat, we can resume our tour of the warehouses of Tel Aviv."

Watching out of the corner of his eye at Felipe scowling at their driver, Daniel had to admit he was rather enjoying Moshe's breezy sarcasm. If anything, it made him look at what they were doing. Seeking an apartment in a foreign city, they hoped one would resonate with them.

"Yes," Daniel answered, causing Felipe's eyes to snap over in his direction. "I think it's fair to say we could all stand to get some food in us."

With that, Moshe veered off the main road, following one narrow alleyway after another. It led them into the Neve Tzedek neighborhood, which appeared to be a burgeoning arts district. The effect of it was not unlike stumbling from a dark room to one bathed in fluorescent light.

The air burst with summery scents of jasmine and orange blossoms. Spirited Hebrew folk music drifted from open windows. Three-story murals stared out from concrete walls. Precious stones scintillated in homemade jewelry being handed from street vendors to customers who, themselves, were dressed like works of art—crochet tops in the colors of lakes and sunsets, linen suits, flaring lace skirts, oversized, bright satin bows, sandals revealing perfectly tanned feet.

Moshe pulled up in front of a brick-red café whose facade hosted sculpture work that made it look as though mythological beasts were emerging from the wall itself. They could smell the fresh coffee and thick spices the moment they flung open the car doors. Inside, the air buzzed with the hypnotic rhythm of a darbuka drum and the soulful melodies of an oud.

When Daniel—known to wolf down a meal even when he was much less hungry than he was after a day of fruitless apartment hunting—finished well before Felipe and Moshe, he began strolling the café, his eyes scanning the paintings on various sizes of canvases that decorated every wall completely. Under each was a small, centered placard that shared detailed about the artist, written first in Hebrew, then in English.

It was easy to pick up on a recurring theme: many of the artists were Holocaust survivors, their artwork tinkering with light and dark, rubble and construction, charred earth and new vegetation in a way that roared into Daniel's consciousness.

These were not subtle paintings; there was no call for them to be. They were confrontational, survivors' songs writ in oil paint. Daniel's eyes lingered on scene after scene after scene that all seemed to whisper, "Life goes on."

One painting in particular caught his eye. It was a dark and brooding landscape dominated by a twisted tree silhouetted against a bloodred sky. There were no signs of renewal in this one, and as much as Daniel admired the other painters' themes of perseverance, he quickly found himself backing up anyone's desire to portray the darkness with no obligatory light to balance it.

Lightly touching one corner of the frame, Daniel thought, *It's true to how many of us feel. Earth was ruined, and the heavens filled with blood.*

As though to physically snap out of his own dark thoughts, Daniel retracted his hand from the artwork and clasped it behind his back. This left him in a classically contemplative stance perfect for someone casually examining paintings and the stories behind them. When his eyes fell to the placard, his hands unclasped automatically, falling loose and heavy at his sides.

Meanwhile, at their table, Felipe was chatting with Moshe over glasses of limonana and plates of falafel. His eyes affixed to the front window, which seemed to serve as the café's largest art frame. Felipe expressed his surprise that an arts district was so close to the industrial zone they were just in.

"Yes," Moshe said, "they are like two different worlds. But believe it or not, you can access one from the other even faster than we got here."

"What do you mean?" Felipe asked.

Gesturing broadly toward the back of the café, Moshe answered that it was possible to walk through a small, wooded patch in the back of this place and emerge practically in the backyard of a building at the opposite end of the industrial zone from where they'd been looking last.

"What kind of building?" Felipe asked. "A production building of some sort?"

Moshe shook his head. "On the other end, where we were looking at the yellow apartment building, that's more of a . . . lively area. Families of some power plant workers live there. Then you have the industrial strip itself. Then—right behind us if you know the way—is another residential building, but they're all resident-owned condos and most of them are retirees."

"A retirement community, you would say?" Felipe leaned back in his chair, not certain what to make of the information he was receiving.

"Of sorts. And the footpath from here to there is perfect for them. Not always having to hop in their cars and contend with traffic."

Or a driver's license, Felipe thought. *Or vehicle registration papers. Or the possibility of being stopped by a police officer while driving.*

"Would it be fair to say a lot of the retirees in that building fancy themselves artists?" Even as he was speaking to Moshe, Felipe's eyes cast around for Daniel. When he spotted him, he wondered what it was about that picture of a grotesque-looking tree Daniel found so intriguing.

With a shrug, Moshe wiped sauce from his final bite of falafel off his mouth and surrounding beard.

"I couldn't say. Stands to reason, but I think for a lot them, they appreciate looking at the art or they just want to have their privacy and be close to where things are happening."

Out of the corner of his eye, Felipe could see Daniel discreetly lifting a camera to snap a picture of the tree painting, of the placard beneath it.

"I don't know too much about it," Moshe continued. "This is lining up something with you? Seems like you are finding this of interest."

"The man who recommended the building we're looking for . . ." Felipe began, choosing his words carefully. "He would be retirement age."

"And is an artist?"

Felipe fought to keep the derision out of his voice as he said, "He thinks of himself as one . . . Would it be possible for Daniel and I to explore the path and meet you back here?"

Moshe, who had been paid in advance—and handsomely—for the whole day, flashed Felipe a smile.

"Have I mentioned the hamantaschen here?" He gestured toward a display case at the front filled with, among rows of other goodies, triangle-shaped cookies that appeared to be brimming with jam.

"They have one that's chocolate and raspberry with orange zest," Moshe gushed.

"Is that your way of saying you'll be fine waiting?" Felipe laughed.

"I will see you gentlemen later. If you find your friend and decide to visit a long time, let me know, or I will eat my way through the entire bakery case."

~~~

On the footpath between the café where their driver was filling himself with fruit-sweetened pastries in an area that was possible Hitler now called home, Daniel began telling Felipe about the painting of the dark tree against its violent backdrop.

"I saw you staring at that one," Felipe said. "It looks nightmarish. What is it about this one?"

"Otto Schwartz," Daniel answered. "Does that name mean anything to you?"

Felipe shook his head. "Never heard of him."

"Neither have I. And I wouldn't have thought anything of it, except his painting is so different than the others, and his artist's placard was kind of . . ."

"What?"

"I took a picture of it, but it said something to the effect of Otto's work being shown all over the world, bought up by kings and queens, that sort of thing."

"Sounds a bit delusional."

"For a so-so artist showing in a café, I'd say."

"So there's a local painter pretending to be a big deal. What are you thinking, Daniel?"

Daniel's eyes widened. "I'm thinking his signature had a very familiar slant to it."

The duo was already almost at the point where trees gave way to the open lawn behind a monolith of concrete and glass.

The building was out of the way. With the footpath from the arts district quietly tucked away, the only likely passersby were power plant and warehouse workers—creatures of routine, unlikely to spare the familiar apartment building a second glance. It was secluded, but not so out of the way as to scream "hiding place." It was well positioned, but it wasn't obvious. These are things Hitler would've thought about.

He also would have thought about what the topography proffered in terms of landscapes waiting to be painted. What could be better for a lonely old man who imagined himself to be an unfairly rejected artist than licking his wounds between an arts district in his backyard and, to the front of the building—which Felipe and Daniel now found themselves gazing upon—a long, serene, gurgling river.

"You think Otto Schwartz is Adolf Hitler?" Felipe asked, no more alarm in his voice than if he'd been asking for directions to the bank or for Daniel's opinion on the weather that afternoon.

"I think this is one of the only places in Israel he would consider good enough for him," Daniel answered, shielding his eyes as he looked toward the top tiers of the building.

"I think he wouldn't hesitate to claim his sketches caused bidding wars among royals."

As the two men walked around to the front of the building, the parking lot's hot pavement burned through the soles of their shoes. The air buzzed with machine sounds. Felipe retrieved his own camera and began snapping photos of the building from different angles.

He was so focused on the tinted windows dotting upper-floor apartments that he didn't notice the three stern-faced men in dark suits approaching.

"Excuse me," one of the men said, his voice sharp. "This is private property. You're not allowed to take pictures here."

"I apologize," Felipe said. "I didn't realize."

The man stepped closer, his eyes scanning Felipe up and down. "You're not from around here, are you?" he asked.

"No," Felipe admitted. "I'm visiting from Argentina."

"And what brings you to this part of town?" the man inquired.

Felipe hesitated for a moment, then said, "I heard there was an excellent retirement community in this area. My grandmother is looking for a place to live, and I wanted to take some pictures to show her."

The man's expression softened slightly. "Ah, I see," he said. "Well, you've come to the right place. This is indeed a retirement community, and a very good one at that."

"I'm glad to hear it," Felipe said. "I'm sure my grandmother would be happy here. The security seems quite vigilant."

The man nodded. "We've had some troublemakers trying to break in recently," he explained. "We have to be careful."

"I understand," Felipe said. "It's good to know that the residents are well-protected."

Felipe gestured to Daniel, who was hanging back and watching the exchange with interest.

"This is my cousin," Felipe said. "He's also interested in seeing the community."

The man introduced himself as Habib, and his companions as Amir and Karim. He explained that there were no vacancies at the moment, and that any tours would have to be arranged in advance.

Felipe's mind raced. They couldn't leave empty-handed after coming all this way. He needed to get inside, to see the layout, assess the security. A plan began to form.

"Actually,"—Felipe snapped his fingers as though he'd just remembered something—"one of my mother's friends lives here. I think her name is . . . Miriam. Yes, Miriam Cohen. She's in apartment 309, I believe." He held his breath, hoping the number wasn't already taken.

Habib frowned. "I don't believe that's the name of the resident in 309."

Felipe feigned disappointment. "Oh my, I must have gotten the apartment number wrong. It was so long ago." He turned to Daniel. "Perhaps we should just come back another time, after we've confirmed with Grandmother."

Daniel didn't miss a beat as he played along. "Yes, it's probably best not to disturb anyone without an invitation."

Habib nodded curtly. "That would be wise. We've had enough disturbances lately."

On one hand, Felipe knew that they'd harvested a great deal of detail today, and that it wouldn't be a bad thing to have Moshe drive them back to their hotel where he and Daniel could plan in earnest. On the other hand, he couldn't help but feel the sickening sense of an opportunity slipping away.

"Would it be possible to just go up quickly and knock on the door?" Felipe pressed. "I wouldn't want to leave without saying hello if she's home."

Amir, the youngest of the three guards, spoke up. "I'm afraid that's not possible. Due to the recent break-ins, we've been instructed not to allow any unauthorized visitors inside the building."

Felipe's heart sank, but he maintained his facade. "Of course, I understand. Security is paramount. We'll come back another time, properly prepared."

He extended his hand to Habib. "Thank you for your time. It's a lovely community."

Habib shook his hand, his eyes still narrowed in suspicion. "You're welcome. Feel free to return when you've obtained clearance from a resident and they've notified us it's acceptable for you to enter."

Felipe and Daniel returned to the café, where Moshe was currently sitting back in his chair with eyes half closed, simply enjoying the waves of folk music and allowing pastries to digest. The moment they were deposited back at the hotel, Felipe turned to Daniel.

"Did you see anything useful?" he asked.

Daniel nodded. "I think so. There's a side entrance that doesn't seem to be as heavily guarded. And the back of the building, as we've seen, is mostly obscured by trees. It might be possible to get in that way."

Felipe grinned. "We'll come back after dark and get a closer look?"

Daniel shook his head at Felipe, though not without endearment. He couldn't help but appreciate his companion's child-like excitement at new clues on the hunt for this monster.

"Probably," he said. "But there's something we need to do first."

~~~

The Mossad headquarters in Tel Aviv was a fortress of concrete and steel, a testament to the constant vigilance that had kept Israel safe for decades. No matter how long Daniel stayed away, he knew its corridors and offices like memories of his childhood neighborhood—at a level that felt like instinct. However, this time his absence had been a long one. New faces hovered over thick mahogany desks. New voices spoke intrusively and sternly into receivers that carried commands to field agents who would, no doubt, hear them as gospel.

The director's office was as austere as Daniel remembered, the walls bare save for a framed photograph of David Ben-Gurion, Israel's first prime minister. The director himself, a lean, sharp-eyed man named Eli Cohen, rose from behind his desk as they entered.

"Daniel," he greeted, a flicker of surprise crossing his face. "And . . ."

"Felipe," Daniel supplied, not averted his eyes from Eli nor producing any discernible expression.

"To what do I owe this unexpected visit?"

With a warmer tone issued by a warmer man, the words may have sounded inviting and encouraged Daniel and Felipe to relax—arrange themselves comfortably in Eli's stuffed leather furnishings and shoot the breeze before they delved into the rather staggering news of what brought them here.

Eli wasn't warm by nature, but that was doubly true when it came to dealing with Daniel Lavy, whom he remembered primarily as an agent too rogue even for Mossad. What Eli was really asking, in other words, was, "What the hell are you doing here, Daniel?"

Daniel, always game for cutting to the chase, said the words he knew would make Eli balk: "We have reason to believe that Hitler is alive and living in Tel Aviv."

For what felt like far longer than a few ticking seconds, the only movement came from Eli's eyebrows. They rose high and stayed put. Then his eyes shifted from Daniel's face to Felipe's, checking whether Daniel's second-in-command was going to back up this preposterous claim.

"We have evidence," Felipe interjected. "There's a heavily-guarded apartment building in Buenos Aires that's occupied by a woman we strongly believe to be Gretl Braun—and Nils Hoffman, son of Heinrich Hoffmann, the photographer—"

"I know who Hoffmann is." Cohen interrupted. He kept his volume low, but his breed of quiet had an effect very similar to if he'd yelled and slammed his fists on the table.

Warned but not deterred, Felipe pressed on. "The building has top-notch security and is openly suspicious of anyone sneaking around. Most of the residents appear to be native Germans who have assumed new identities. And there's a woman in the penthouse of that apartment building who's been receiving mail from someone named Klaus—"

"And Klaus is who?" Cohen had taken to leaning on his desk, knuckles pressed to wood. He looked up at Felipe beneath angled brows.

Daniel found it wise to field this one. "A dead-end unto himself. But clearly someone with information. He's been writing to the woman in the penthouse about their 'mutual friend' who lives in Israel."

Felipe made a noise like he wanted to jump in, but Daniel was on a role, and—quite frankly—he didn't want Cohen to sink his canines into Felipe the way he was likely to do to whomever laid out the rest of their findings. "The description in the letters led us to investigate apartment buildings in industrial zones of Tel Aviv."

"Led. As in this is something you've already done."

"Rather than come to you with nothing,"—*so you could say as much and throw us out*, Daniel added silently—"yes, we investigated on our own. We hired a driver and searched every industrial apartment complex until we found one next to an arts district across from a river— supposedly full of retirees— yet guarded by a security detail you wouldn't want to run into in a dark alley."

Felipe pled Daniel to "tell him about the painting," so Daniel told Eli why he believed Adolf Hitler was now going by the name Otto Schwartz, which was answered by a jeering laugh from Cohen.

"Otto Schwartz?"

"He would've adopted a name to try to fit in," Daniel said sternly. "It makes sense."

At this point, Cohen collapsed back into his stuffed leather chair, which groaned under his sudden weight. Abandoning his typical authoritative stature, he sat with his left arm sprawled loosely across his desktop, his shoulders leaned back against the chair, and his right hand on his lap in a sort of cupped position, as though he had been holding an object that was been snatched away from him.

"If he wanted to fit in," Cohen started, "he's done a hell of a job. Do you know how many Otto Schwartz there likely are scattered all through Israel?"

Felipe found himself taking short, shallow breaths to calm himself. He was growing sick of both Cohen's obtuseness and his exaggerated show of frustration with them. What he *wanted* to say was, "Sorry Hitler didn't make himself easier to find." Instead, he said nothing; he deferred to Daniel, who told Cohen, "Even if there are a million, we need to see if there's one who lives in that building and, if so, have a chit-chat with him about his opinions on Jewish people."

"A few seconds ago, you claimed you had evidence," Cohen said abruptly. "From what I understand, your evidence consists of letters from someone with a common German name about someone else with a common German name, sent to the penthouse occupant of an apartment building where you believe Gretl Braun and, for some reason, Heinrich Hoffmann's son are living under assumed identities."

"Along with a great deal of circumstantial—"

"And may I assume," Cohen said, as he took up the laid-back posture of a man watching his sworn enemy squirm, "that you're keeping your references to the woman in the penthouse very vague because you have no idea who she is?"

"We have her name," Felipe said, as calmly as he could. It was beginning to feel like a conversation between Cohen and himself; not only because they'd been last to speak, but also because Daniel's attention was obviously elsewhere. He was looking out the window so intently that Felipe followed his gaze—he saw nothing outside except a sparrow whose flittering movement made it appear jittery, anxious.

For his part, Cohen didn't seem to notice that he was now essentially alone with Felipe.

"Let's have it."

"It's Romilda Lehmann," Felipe said, more hesitantly than he liked. "We believe that to be a false identity."

Cohen chuckled. "Of course you do."

His stance indicated that he was about to open the door and ask them to depart.

"It sounds like you believe everyone's identity to be false. And all these people are living under made-up names with no connections to their old lives. They're all going to lead us to each other, I suppose?"

At that point, much to Felipe's relief, Daniel seemed to re-join them in the room.

"If Hitler is alive and we do nothing, it will be a stain on Mossad's honor."

At this, Cohen visibly bristled. He didn't like Daniel Lavy, that much was known to all and impossible to hide. But he owed him the professional courtesy earned by any agent who had spent years putting his life on the life to protect Israel. He felt he was doing an exemplary job of extending that courtesy at the moment—and here Daniel was making him culpable for dishonoring Mossad.

"Israel is the last place Hitler would ever show his face." Every word Cohen said was clipped, precise.

Felipe couldn't help himself. "We don't even know if he's showing his face! We have reason to believe—"

"Not now," Daniel cut him off. Yes, they had reason to be-lieve that Hitler may have substantially altered his appearance. The intercepted letters hinted at it, as did common sense. Of course he would change his appearance. But Daniel also knew that bringing up plastic surgery wasn't the way to get Cohen to take this seriously.

"Eli," Daniel said, "taken together, the evidence we have is substantial. Pick it apart all you want—but you can't ignore it."

Cohen shook his head. "I'm not ignoring it, I'm simply being realistic. This is the kind of wild goose chase that could cost Mossad dearly. We can't afford to waste our resources on something so unlikely."

The tension in the room was palpable. Daniel could feel his anger rising, but he fought to keep his voice calm.

"Then the consequence of that will fall on your head. When the truth comes out—and it will—Mossad will be held accountable."

Cohen's face hardened. "Don't threaten me, Daniel. I've been running Mossad for years, and I won't be lectured by a rogue agent."

The two men's methods and personalities had always clashed like flint and steel. Daniel knew that—knew their contentious fit had the potential to derail the whole investigation. He'd tried to keep that much in mind. And he felt he'd been reasonable. He also felt Cohen hadn't.

"I'm not threatening you, Eli," Daniel said, his voice now low and dangerous. "I'm warning you. This is your chance to do the right thing. Don't squander it."

"Get out of my office, Daniel," Cohen said, forgoing the civil host's gesture of walking guests to the door. "You and your partner are no longer welcome here."

~~~

As they walked down the corridor, Felipe turned to Daniel, shock and disappointment battling for control of his expression.

"What now, Daniel? What do we do?"

He chose not to interrogate Daniel about where he'd gone mentally back there, when Cohen was on the attack.

Daniel paused at a window in the hallway. His gaze was brief this time—a quick, foggy glance at the bustling city below, and then he was back. He sounded certain of himself when he said, "We keep going. We find Hitler. We bring him to justice."

His voice was quiet, but the determination in his eyes was unmistakable. He would not be deterred, not by Mossad's intransigence, and certainly not by the personal animosity of its director. This tangible commitment was something Felipe had taken comfort in many times in the past and did now as well. For Daniel, this was nothing less than a personal mission—and Daniel Lavy on a mission was a force to be reckoned with.

CHAPTER SIXTEEN

The ballroom of the opulent Hotel Alvear Palace in Buenos Aires was a symphony of cream and gold. A constellation of chandeliers cast a warm glow on the tables below, draped in white linen and dotted with vases of fragrant lilies. The air thrummed with anticipation of a big event just around the corner. And indeed, Giselle couldn't believe it was already time: Karen's wedding would take place the next day.

Resplendent in the moonlight-white dress she was still wearing from the rehearsal, Karen paced the curved lines flowing between tables, brow furrowed in concentration. Giselle wasn't accustomed to seeing her like this. So dressed up, for one thing, but also this anxious.

Throughout the wedding preparations, Karen sidestepped the insidious tensions known to overtake brides—the desire to create a memorable, happy day hardening into pressure for perfection.

Giselle couldn't help remembering how she had felt that pressure herself—though only briefly. In her case, thanks to where she was in life at the time, it was easy enough to relinquish her anxieties about things she couldn't control and, instead, to lean on God.

It had been late summer in Buenos Aires—the air humid but also alive with promise—when Giselle had stood before the ornate Ark of the Covenant in a high-ceilinged synagogue, her hand clasped in Felipe's. She remembered the stained glass windows casting a kaleidoscope of colors on the white marble floor as the couple stood bathed in a soft, ethereal glow.

They met the rabbi through Daniel, who seemed to know every other person in Buenos Aires despite being, as far as Giselle had ever seen, reasonably hermetic. This rabbi had sung Daniel's praises to the rafters and then stood reciting the Aliyah blessing in his rich and resonant voice. When she looked at Felipe—who was huddled at the Torah with her as God was called to bless their union—he looked like his heart might fly out of his chest.

Then came the Mi Shebeirach blessing, a prayer for healing and protection. Giselle found herself more or less experiencing the blessing's gifts in real time as the rabbi's melodic words flooded her with a serenity she could not, in that moment, imagine ever dissolving. She felt a deep connection to her faith, a certainty that God had a plan for her and Felipe.

Their beaming guests had then showered the couple with candies, soft enough to be welcomed rather than dodged, to symbolize wishes for a sweet life together. She had caught the mischievous twinkle in Felipe's eye a split second before he popped one of the candies into his mouth, then leaned down to kiss Giselle deeply. Their guests' appreciative laughter had mingled with their own, and Giselle remembered that amidst all the merriment, she had the crystal clear thought that "this is what happiness sounds like."

Her heart ached with the memory of the sugar from Felipe's mouth lingering sweetly in her own. What a feeling it had been for her, having both her husband-to-be and her faith reach such a high, merging so seamlessly that it seemed almost silly to think of the important parts of her life as separate.

Here is what had become clear to Giselle in that moment: her life was not arranged in such a way that her marriage was over here, her friendships and relationships with her family over there, her kinship with God in a different spot altogether.

It all beat to the same pulse. There was only what was meant to be, and all that was required of her was to move forward in firm belief and appreciation.

The birth of Elena had only strengthened her faith. Giselle would forever remember marveling at the tiny baby in her arms in the hospital with Felipe at her side, her uncle Daniel pacing in the hallway outside as he attempted to exercise patience to allow the young family to relish their time together.

But she had to admit that as the years passed, doubt had darkened the edges of her faith. It was hard to pinpoint any exact turning point, but she found herself feeling isolated in a way that she never had when her faith was fully in bloom. Giselle had never consciously turned away from God, but her prayers had become less frequent, her belief less resolute.

Presently, the weight of her secrets, the knowledge of the darkness that lurked beneath the surface of her seemingly perfect life, had cast a pall over her spirit. She longed for the simple faith that, in her youth, had convinced her everything would be alright in the end—that if she did the right thing, benevolence would befall her and her loved ones in the long term.

It was comical that gazing upon the bride-to-be of a family allegedly entrenched in the vilest acts against Jews would provide the impetus for Giselle's thoughts to linger softly on the religion of her youth. She had never stopped fighting for it, of course—not simply as a religion, but as a culture, a heritage, a host of rites passed down through blood—but she had not paused in quite some time to reflect on what Judaism was to her personally.

The way Karen was looking at Giselle snapped her back to the present. She realized she had been adrift in her reveries for some time.

She smiled at Karen.

"You look beautiful," Giselle said.

Karen returned the smile, her eyes sparkling with gratitude.

"Thank you, Giselle. And thank you for being by my side today. God knows what kind of state I'd be in without you." In her chuckle was a note of light self-deprecation.

It wouldn't be the last time that day Giselle's thoughts drifted back to her own special day. But even as she luxuriated in vivid memories of the chuppah, the scent of the lilies, and the sweetness of the candies, she knew she could never share these memories with Karen. Their weddings, like their lives, were shaped by two very different histories and experiences of what it was to be a modern young woman in the late-1960s. The rift between them couldn't be bridged—only acknowledged and exploited to bring about justice.

Giselle knew all of that. So why was she so tempted, right then, to offer Karen advice from the lens of someone who'd been through this before? To tell her she'd feel a million times better approximately halfway down the aisle, at which point it would hit her that the time for preparations had expired, and the time to ceremonially start her new life had begun. To tell Karen that she would be okay and to mean it?

~~~

The muted hum of the air conditioner filled the silence of the hotel room, a sharp contrast to the vibrant energy of Tel Aviv pulsing just beyond the window. Daniel sat on the edge of the bed, his gaze fixed on a carpet pattern that was ornate but faded from years of exposure to both sunlight and the socked feet of excited Tel Aviv tourists. Felipe adjusted the curtain to hide a sliver of brightness leaking through when he discovered the heaviness of the curtains. They felt like a material denser than cloth. Or maybe he was just exhausted.

He could certainly see that Daniel was.

Perching himself on the armchair by the window, Felipe watched his friend with a mixture of concern and curiosity.

"You've been distant lately, Daniel," he began, his voice gentle but not wavering. He was voicing something that had dropped an anchor in his mind before they ever left for Israel: even back in his family's kitchen, Felipe had observed Daniel's long, vacant stares into nothingness. Sometimes he or Giselle, or even Elena, would have to repeat something three times before Daniel seemed to realize he was being spoken to.

That wasn't the case this time, however. Felipe managed to snag Daniel's attention in one line. Daniel looked up, his eyes mirroring some inner turmoil that Felipe increasingly feared signified a reluctance about their investigation. Sure, Daniel still stood by his side—tenacious, when necessary—but that didn't mean he didn't harbor misgivings.

As he had done many times in their history together, Daniel seemed to read Felipe's mind.

"It's not that I've lost faith in our mission," he said in a measured voice. "But I admit I've been reflecting on Judd's words, his warnings about the cost of this obsession."

Felipe nodded. "He does have a way of putting things, doesn't he?"

This was framing it mildly, Felipe knew, but he still felt hesitant to give much leeway to Judd's arguments because he didn't fully understand what the man's intentions were. On paper, Felipe and Judd agreed about this mission: capture Hitler if possible, but proceed with caution. But Felipe couldn't shake the feeling that, in a sense, they were coming from two entirely different places.

"He does," Daniel agreed with a wry smile. "But I think he's right. We've been so focused on finding Hitler that we haven't given much thought to what comes after. What happens to us, to our families, once this is all over?"

Felipe's brow furrowed. "What do you mean?"

Daniel sighed, his shoulders slumping in a way they typically only did toward the end of the day, when exhaustion and three or four whiskeys caught up with him.

"I'm worried, Felipe. I'm worried that we'll be so consumed by this pursuit that we'll lose sight of what truly matters. Our loved ones. Our own basic ability to live our lives."

He paused, his gaze drifting toward the framed photograph on the nightstand. Ever since Paraguay, he'd made a habit of bringing this picture with him wherever he traveled. He immediately positioned it a place he could see easily when he drifted off at night and when he woke in the mornings. It was a picture of his twin sons, their faces filled with an innocent youthfulness that had reappeared in flickers but not a steady flame since they had been imprisoned in Hitler's compound alongside so many other children.

"I don't want to end up like that," Daniel continued, his voice uncharacteristically thick with emotion. "I don't want you and Giselle to, either."

Even as he referred to himself and Felipe, his eyes remained trained on his sons. There was no doubt who occupied his mind as he finished, "I don't want any of us to lose sight."

Felipe remained silent for a moment, his mind racing. He had always been the more optimistic one of the two, the one who believed in the power of hope and the triumph of good over evil.

Daniel's words addressed a latent concern. He knew he'd been defensive when it was Judd delineating these warning signs, but that was because he feared Judd's overall message was "let this go." Felipe heard Daniel in a way he hadn't been able to hear Judd—openly —mentee listening to mentor.

"You're right," Felipe finally said. "I've been so fixated on finding Hitler that I haven't considered the aftermath. The scars this will leave on us, on our children."

He thought of Elena, his beloved daughter, her laughter echoing in the empty apartment back home. Of course, she was never far from his thoughts. But when he thought of his paternal responsibility to her, he tended to see only one demon from which he needed to shield her: Hitler himself. The understanding was settling in with him now, new and uncomfortable, that she stood to inherit burdens beyond living in a world in which Adolf Hitler had not been eliminated yet. She would also be affected by her family's day-and-night obsession with the man.

For a moment—one of these moments capable of mimicking an hour—Felipe was plagued with the vision of Elena growing up with the sense that, as long as some monster loomed in the distance, her life could never really start. He saw her living dimly, looking at life from behind a sort of filmy glass not present in her youth.

When he shook himself out of what he could only regard as a vision of doom, Felipe saw the way Daniel examined a now-old photograph of his sons, and he felt the two of them were likely thinking similar things.

"I haven't asked about your sons lately," Felipe said. "How are they coping with all of this?"

"They're . . . struggling."

With that, Daniel stopped gazing at the picture frame, finding it too much to speak the words aloud while looking square at their faces.

"The trauma of Paraguay still haunts them. They have nightmares, panic attacks. Claudia is doing her best, but it's a constant battle."

A wave of guilt washed over him. He had rescued his sons from Hitler's clutches, and it had been the most worthwhile effort and happiest triumph of his life. But he thought about it now so differently than he had then.

When Hitler's comrades were being interrogated and dragged away to prison, and the world was focused on spreading the news of Hitler and Eva Braun's escape—so a worldwide network could have its collective eyes peeled for the terrorist fugitives—Daniel had no room to feel anything but overjoyed that his sons were alive. Overjoyed that their mission had at least been successful in the sense of shutting the compound down and freeing the caged children that were experimented on like lab rats. Looking back, he realized the relief of that moment had contrasted so sharply with everything before that he had mistaken the moment for a more conclusive resolution than it truly was.

He hadn't been able to see, from the vantage point of Paraguay, how the hours, the weeks, the years that followed would seem to keep offering his boys, and by extension, himself, fresh wounds.

"I wish there was something I could do," Daniel mumbled.

Felipe nodded.

"I know the feeling," he said. "I often have nightmares about Elena being one of those children in Paraguay."

The ticking of a clock, which incorrectly reported the time as 6:15 p.m., filled the room as they both sat with the knowledge that evil's aftershocks live on long after the perpetrators have been jailed. Felipe felt that, for the first time, he could not only understand but appreciate Judd's apparent pushback against this mission.

It wasn't that he didn't want them to succeed, or didn't understand the importance of detaining Hitler and his henchmen by any means necessary—he had just been in war situations long enough to have witnessed, over and over again, the way its shadow continues to ravage the mind. Felipe had assumed that, for whatever strange reason, Judd couldn't understand his overwhelming instinct to protect his daughter and wife from a tyrant willing to destroy them blindly. Now he understood that Judd simply knew capturing Hitler was never going to be completely under their control—that if one little thing went wrong and the man fled, Felipe stood to spend the rest of his life chasing vapor while his little girl grew up.

With a few heavy blinks, Felipe rejoined the present moment. No sooner did the thought occur to him than he was saying it out loud: "There is something we can do, Daniel."

He was on his feet before he realized it. "We can help those children, the ones who were trapped in that compound. We can make sure they get the support they need to heal, to rebuild their lives."

Daniel betrayed no emotion beyond frank curiosity.

"What do you have in mind?"

Felipe outlined his plan, his voice growing more animated with each word. They could use Daniel's vast resources to fund a program that would provide counseling, therapy, and educational opportunities for the children and their families. They could partner with local organizations and experts in trauma recovery to ensure the program was effective and sustainable.

"It's a bold idea, Felipe," Daniel said.

Felipe knew to take the statement as a sort of endorsement. Daniel was nearly always in favor of boldness—he was Felipe's inspiration to override his own various timidities and go big.

Daniel was, it appeared, ready to go big. He paused only long enough to start tabulating the logistics, particularly the financial implications.

"I'll cover the costs," he said decisively. "Whatever it takes."

As Felipe's smile spread, a warmth simultaneously spread across his chest. He added, "But we might need some help. Perhaps we could reach out to the Red Cross. They would know something about setting up efforts like this on a large scale."

Felipe felt a jolt of nervousness watching a shadow fall across Daniel's features.

"The Red Cross?" he asked. "The same Red Cross that gave a leg up to Nazis escaping the war?"

Felipe was honestly surprised he'd skirted this issue in his own mind before suggesting it. He wasn't in the dark about Daniel's feelings on this or any other organization he viewed, in the slightest, as Nazi Helpers. Although Felipe didn't blame Daniel, he felt hopeful about his idea and its singular promise of recovery that not even capturing the biggest-name villains would immediately bring. That he could rally for building alliances to take it from a good idea to a working program.

"But they've also done a lot of good in the world," he said. "Maybe it's time we focused on the good, Daniel."

Daniel considered his friend's words. Perhaps Felipe was right. After all, it wasn't an entirely different message from the one Judd had been championing and Daniel himself had adopted. Perhaps it was time to let go of the anger and resentment that had fueled their pursuit for so long.

He reached out and briefly clasped Felipe's hand. They would find Hitler—they would bring him to justice. But they would also honor the victims, the survivors, and the children whose lives had been forever scarred by the horrors of the past.

They would not let the darkness consume them.

CHAPTER SEVENTEEN

"**K**aren!" Giselle called with a soft laugh, as she watched her friend hover over one of the round, cloth-covered tables holding the same two bone-white miniature name placards she had moved twice already. "Everything is perfect!"

Karen stopped her pacing and turned to face Giselle, a nervous smile playing on her lips. "Easy for you to say. You're not the one juggling a guest list full of potential time bombs."

Giselle chuckled. "Oh, I'm well aware of the challenges of the family seating chart," she said. "It's hard enough to make a peaceful seating chart when you're only working with one family—but when you've got your own and your in-laws . . . trust me, everything will be fine. People are generally on their best behavior at weddings."

Karen sighed. "Hans's family is a breeze compared to mine. Some of the most mild-mannered Germans I've ever met."

A spontaneous laugh arose from Giselle. "Somehow I could see Hans coming from a mild-mannered family."

"I'm telling you."

With another sigh, Karen set down the place cards, going so far as to playfully flick one of them onto its back.

"You know, I love that about him. My mother doesn't get it—*at all*. To her, any man worth feeling something for, and certainly getting married to must be"—Karen donned a thick German accent, the one Giselle had heard come out of Lotte only after she'd had numerous cocktails—"exciting and passionate and strong!"

Laughing, Giselle smoothed out a tablecloth edge that had become rumpled from the numerous times Karen's dress had brushed it in her pacing. "Not your type, huh?"

"I had that kind of thing with Wolfgang. And yeah, exciting for a minute I guess, but . . ."

As she always did in these conversations, Giselle walked the tightrope. She was talking to her best friend about an ex-fiancé. She was also talking to Hitler's niece about a former lover who was probably "exciting" in the precise way the most heavily-armed person in the room always is. She was discussing, on the eve of her friend's wedding, the silliness of some family members who regarded romance as a storybook affair deserved only by heroic, larger-than-life men. She was exploring the romantic inclinations of a woman who'd borne a child with a high-ranking Nazi official and, if she read Karen's voice correctly, may have had a crush on Karen's uncle all the while.

Giselle rubbed a tender place on her forehead. "But what?" she said, instantly afraid she'd said it more curtly than she should have.

If Giselle's tone had encapsulated the slightest irritation, Karen missed it in her own preoccupations. She surprised Giselle when she said, "But . . . he wasn't a nice man."

Giselle's breath hitched. A lump she had to swallow without showing that something in this simple statement had thrown her off deeply. She furrowed her brow a bit, on purpose. She turned to Karen wearing a mask of concern.

"He was mean to you?"

Karen looked away. "No." Then her eyes found Giselle's again. "He was just . . . mean. Generally. If I'm being honest, there's a streak of it that runs in my family, and for a long time, I suppose I thought . . . that's the way of things. That's how life goes, that's how men are, that's how people are."

Her fingers again played at the nearest place cards, and when she looked away this time, it was because her eyelashes had dampened with tears.

"That's why . . . it's just all hitting me now. Now that I'm arranging them around these nice tables for my wedding."

Doing her best to keep her breath as well as her thoughts steady, Giselle squeezed Karen's hand.

"Why don't you tell me who you're most worried about? Maybe I can help you strategize."

Karen hesitated, a flicker of doubt crossing her face. "I don't know, Giselle. It's complicated."

"Complicated how?"

Karen took a deep breath, as if steeling herself for a confession. "Some of the people on my list . . . let's just say they have history."

Giselle's heart quickened. On one hand, a family that overlapped with Hitler's bloodline would have history to say the least. On the other, every family in the world had history—and weddings brought it out. Distant relatives that sat next to each other for big, emotional events were bound to tap into each other's bottled-up angst, irritation, and disapproval, among other things. That was the situation of every family, as a group of individuals with shared memories and differing tastes.

Conversely, every family had a history, and weddings tended to bring them to the forefront.

What frustrated Giselle so much was that she still found herself on the fence when it came to Karen. She was decided about everyone else. But still Giselle found herself continually combing through the details of their friendship and of her team's case against Karen simultaneously.

"What kind of history?" she asked, giving the question a light tone and casual shrug as though to say—*c'mon Karen, welcome to having a family.*

Karen glanced around the ballroom. She let her eyes linger on the stray centerpiece here and chandelier there, but Giselle clearly understood it as a cover-up for checking to make sure they were alone.

Giselle stepped closer, her eyes locking with Karen's.

"Karen. I'm your maid of honor. I'm here for you, no matter what. You can trust me."

Karen studied Giselle's face, searching for any sign of deceit or hesitation. At least that's how Giselle interpreted the depth of Karen's close-range stare. She felt its heaviness along with a separate one weighing on her chest.

With a smile, she cracked the unbearable tension, for both of them.

"Let's play a game."

Karen titled her head. "A game?"

"Yes." Giselle could practically feel the mischievous glint in her eyes, perhaps because she saw it reflecting in Karen's.

"Let's go through the room, table by table. You tell me who's sitting where, and we'll imagine the worst possible scenario. And I, as your bridesmaid, will help you come up with solutions for any bad apples."

Giselle was relieved to see humor flood back into Karen's eyes.

"I have to tell you—I was so hoping the game was going to be poker. Like you were just going to say, let's get out of here, find a live poker game going somewhere, blow off some steam . . ."

Giselle laughed. "When you're a happily-married lady, you can play all the poker you want. Let's play this slightly more boring game for now, to get you there."

Their footsteps en route to the first table were muffled by the plush pearl-colored carpet. The center of the floor itself was bare for dancing, but the parameter, meant for seating, was carpeted in a way that made Giselle think *winter wonder-land*. Karen pointed to the first name on the seating chart.

~~~

The air inside the surveillance van was thick with the metallic tang of electronics and the musk of five men crammed into a space meant for three. Colonel Judd hunched over a bank of monitors, eyes glued to the live feed from Giselle's hidden camera. The grainy image on the screen showed Karen and Giselle pacing the opulent ballroom, their voices quiet in the otherwise silent space.

"Jefferson," Judd barked, his voice raspy from years of shouting orders on the parade ground. "Get your pen ready. We need every name Karen mentions."

Jefferson, a wiry man with skin like a rumpled blanket and tufty gray hair, nodded eagerly, his eyes sparkling with excitement. Of the many feats the former intelligence analyst was proud of, his legendary penmanship ranked high on the list. In his gnarled hand, a simple ballpoint pen became weaponized.

"Miguel," Judd continued, his gaze never leaving the screen. "Start cross-referencing those names against the tenant list from Lotte and Nils's building."

Miguel, a dark-haired man with a youthful energy that belied his sixty-some-odd years, tapped his pen so furiously against the Steno notepads in his lap that the writing instrument blurred in motion.

"Hammerhead," Judd said, turning to the hulking figure in the corner. "Check those names against the guest list from Lotte's birthday party."

Hammerhead, a man of few words and even fewer smiles, grunted in acknowledgement. He was a former Marine sniper, his eyesight as sharp as his reflexes. Thanks to his steel-trap memory, he could recall every detail of a conversation or even a face.

"Frank," Judd addressed a quiet man in the group with a neatly-trimmed mustache. "Cross-reference those names with our database of Hitler's known associates."

Frank, a methodical and meticulous researcher, nodded silently, his eyes already scanning the list of names on his screen. He had a knack for uncovering hidden connections, for finding the threads that wove together seemingly disparate events.

The van hummed with activity, a symphony of clicking keyboards, whispered commands, and the occasional muttered curse. The tension was as palpable as the stakes were high, but every former Marine in the van was well accustomed to both.

~~~

"First we have my mother," Karen said in a comedic announcer's tone, "known to those not fortunate enough to be her daughter, as 'Lotte.'"

Known to Upper Crust Germany as Gretl Braun? Giselle added silently.

Karen continued, "She'll probably corner some poor waiter and regale him with tales of her glamorous past . . . or complain about the lack of strudel on the dessert table."

"If that's the worst we can expect from her, I'll take it." Giselle chuckled. "So, we make sure the dessert tables are sagging under the weight of strudel, and we tell the waiters their tips depend on oohing and aahing at your mother's stories."

The next few names involved similar troubleshooting: planning for casual *faux pas* based on trends set over a number of years at other parties. Then they came to Nils.

The next few names required troubleshooting, based on years of trends at other parties.

"You remember my cousin?" Karen rolled her eyes.

"Of course," Giselle said. "I remember thinking he was so . . . formal when I met him, but a few drinks at your mother's birthday party loosened him right up. Do you expect any issues there? Think he might blab family secrets or show off some inappropriate dance moves?"

Giselle had to congratulate herself on the construction of this question—how she slipped "blab family secrets" in before the innocence of breaking out embarrassing dance moves. She didn't necessarily expect it to be the question that would finally crack Karen open like a pistachio shell, but she believed her wording made it clear she wasn't assuming that Karen's family secrets were any darker than anyone else's. There was nothing at all in Giselle's tone that let on that she knew Nils was capable of much, much worse than some inappropriate dance moves.

Karen laughed, seeming to imagine her cousin flinging elbows and knees in the ballroom.

"He fancies himself a poet, actually. And his poetry is bad enough when it *isn't* just drunken ramblings."

Giselle's smile tightened. "We'll just have to keep him away from the microphone during the toasts."

Table by table, they worked their way through the guest list, with nearly every revelation about a guest's peculiar foibles bringing about a new spell of laughter.

"And this," Karen said, her voice dropping to a serious tone, "is where the real problems begin."

Giselle's breath caught in her throat. She knew what Karen meant. The remaining names belonged not simply to embarrassing relatives—the likes of which any blushing bride would have—but to relatives whose flaws could not be compensated for by even the best seating chart strategy.

Giselle reached out and took Karen's hand in a firm grip. Her own mind felt like a pot threatening to boil over any second. Karen might as well have held up a sign announcing that she wanted to talk—about everything. This was no time for timidity.

"Karen," Giselle said, "tell me. Whatever it is, whatever seems so bad. It's not going to change how I look at you, okay?"

Karen looked into Giselle's eyes, a flicker of fear and uncertainty warring with the trust she saw reflected back at her.

"Do you really want to know?" Karen asked, her voice barely audible.

CHAPTER EIGHTEEN

A voice crustier than week-old bread emerged from the back of the van.

"All these names you're having us check—most of them are going to be aliases. What's the point?"

It was Johnson, a former demolition expert who would wear the long, jagged scar from a training accident for the rest of his days.

Judd turned to face him, eyes made of steel.

"Most of them will be, you're right. But if we have aliases that match across contexts, it matters. If we have partial matches on real names, it matters. Besides, Karen is on the verge of spilling her guts. Giselle's got her right where we want her. All our girl has to do is play her cards right, and we'll have a taped confession from a member of Hitler's own family."

And that may be all we have, he added silently. The name Romilda Lehmann hadn't come up in the whole guest registry. Tonight, they would get no closer to answering the question of who she really was—or if there was any chance she was actually Eva Braun in disguise. Either she was considered too high-profile and refused to attend an event as public as this one, or she had been tipped off to heightened security risks—perhaps by an investigative team tracking her family. Or maybe she was not Eva Braun and held no significance to Karen's family at all—she was just another resident in the building.

Judd paused, his gaze sweeping across the faces of his colleagues.

"Remember, our mission is to find Hitler. Everything else is secondary. We can't afford to get distracted by side quests. We need to stay focused, stay sharp, and stay one step ahead of the enemy."

His words hung in the air, a reminder of the gravity of their task. The men nodded, their expressions set with grim determination. They were soldiers—trained to follow orders, to execute their mission with ruthless efficiency. But they were also men driven by a thirst for justice, a desire to right the wrongs of the past.

CHAPTER NINETEEN

Night shrouded the Tel Aviv apartment building in an eerie silence, broken only by the rhythmic chirping of crickets and the distant hum of traffic. Under the cover of darkness, Daniel and Felipe crept along the wooded path, their footsteps muffled by the damp earth. The air hung heavy with the scent of pine needles and the tang of the nearby sea.

The back entrance of the building, a nondescript steel door set into a concrete wall, was bathed in the dim glow of a single flickering lightbulb. Daniel produced a lockpick from his pocket, his fingers dancing over the tumblers with practiced ease. A soft click signaled the lock's surrender, and the door creaked open. Behind it, a dimly lit stairwell crawled up and out of view.

Because of their heightened senses, every creak of the floorboards sounded potentially alarming. The air inside the building was stale and musty, with a faint metallic odor that clung to the back of Daniel's throat.

As they reached the second-floor landing, a shadow detached itself from the wall. In better lighting, the shape became a burly figure in a security guard's uniform.

"Halt!" the guard barked. They could clearly make out his meaty hand extending toward his holster.

It was moments like these that reminded Felipe that Daniel was more than the man he appeared to be—an endearingly grouchy but soft-hearted father, uncle, and great-uncle about to fund welfare checks to the traumatized children of Paraguay.

When he needed to be, he was also a combat machine, trained by Mossad as one of its deadliest.

Daniel's fist instantly connected with the guard's jaw in a sickening crunch. The guard fell to the floor immediately, and his eyes rolled back in his head.

"Let's go!"

Daniel wrenched Felipe by the arm toward the nearest apartment door.

They burst into the apartment, guns drawn, adrenaline soaking their nervous systems. Both men's muscles were tense from the impending confrontation.

This apartment was a museum, its furniture shrouded in dust-covered sheets. No one had been there for months. The whole place reeked of neglect.

Felipe's eyes darted from rafters to baseboards.

"Not this one."

Suddenly, the sound of footsteps echoed in the hallway. A sharp click rang out as a gun was cocked.

"Hands up!" a voice commanded.

Daniel and Felipe whirled around with their guns already leveled. Three more grim-faced security guards clotted the doorway. Their own weapons were trained on Daniel and Felipe, and they didn't look like the sort of men who needed an elaborate reason to shoot.

"We're not here to hurt anyone." Daniel's voice sounded calm but firm. "We just want to talk."

The guards didn't so much as exchange glances; their eyes stayed coldly locked on their prey.

"Who are you?" one of them asked, his voice thick with a German accent.

"That's not important," Daniel replied. "What is important is that you let us leave peacefully."

The guard sneered. "I don't think so. You're trespassing, and you assaulted one of my men. You're not going anywhere."

He gestured with his gun, and the guards flanked Daniel and Felipe.

"Don't make this more difficult than it has to be," Felipe warned.

The guard lunged with a fist aimed at Felipe's face. As Felipe ducked, his own fist lashed out in retaliation. The two men grappled, their bodies twisting and turning in a blur of motion.

Daniel, meanwhile, was engaged in a deadly dance with the other two guards. Gunfire erupted—the deafening blasts echoing through the apartment. Daniel felt a searing pain in his shoulder as a bullet grazed his flesh, but he ignored the wound. His sole focus was neutralizing the threat.

He disarmed one guard with a swift kick, then spun around to face the other. But before he could pull the trigger, a gunshot rang out. Then a cry of agony.

Felipe.

With his heart in his throat, Daniel whirled to face his surrogate nephew. Felipe slumped against the wall. Blood slipped through the fingers of his hand that clutched his side.

"Felipe!" Daniel shouted, rushing to his side.

The remaining guards closed in, their guns pointed as one at Daniel's back.

CHAPTER TWENTY

C rystal chandeliers cast dancing reflections on the polished parquet floor at the center of the Hotel Alvear Palace ballroom. A live orchestra, every member fitted in an elegant tuxedo, filled the air with the lively strains of a tango. And out on the dance floor, German couples twirled and dipped and swung with abandon.

The ceremony was over. Hans and Karen were now a proper Mr. & Mrs. The first in their family line was revealed by the slight bump visible beneath Karen's dress.

Resplendent in a sapphire-blue gown that hugged her curves, Giselle watched the scene with a bittersweet smile. Her eyes lingered on Lotte, whose face flushed with excitement as she swayed to the music in the arms of a distinguished-looking gentleman. Nils bounced from one group of guests to another with the energy of a puppy in the park. These two were clearly several drinks in. Giselle monitored them carefully, ready in case either of them became sloppy enough to reveal crucial detail.

Giselle watched Karen's family celebrate, recalling her promise to Karen that morning not to judge her based on her family's actions.

When Karen had still proven reluctant to discuss the details of her family, she was visibly on the verge of tears thinking about them. Giselle had done something that felt somewhat extreme in retrospect, but something she had found herself wanting to attempt as their conversation deepened. She had excused herself to go to the restroom, where she looked in the mirror and said aloud—for Judd's sake—that she was about to call Felipe and needed a little privacy.

On the other end of the mic, Judd's voice had sputtered with the start of questions. She listened just long enough to hear the gist of his objections: He didn't think this was a good time to leave the conversation with Karen hanging. He didn't think it was a good idea to cut the wire. Felipe wouldn't likely be in a place suited for catching up anyway.

She also picked up on the suspicion underlying the specifics of his objections. She had said, in a voice laden with emotion, "Judd, I *have* to have some privacy," and cut the van's feed to her dealings with Karen.

In solitude, she had spent a considerable moment observing herself in the mirror.

Then, with courage built up from the pep talk she had just given her reflection, Giselle walked back up to Karen in the ballroom and asked her, "Have you known all along that I'm Jewish?"

Objectively speaking, the ballroom around them remained cloaked in silence, but both women could've sworn they heard the sound of a hundred vacuums roaring to life. That deafening, that rattling, was the quiet that followed Giselle's question. She was concerned that asking Karen in Judd's presence would not be appropriate, regardless of his opinion on her methods.

No matter how much she wished to deny it, she felt too protective over Karen. It was only alone with her that Giselle could catalyze the real discussion she and Karen needed to have, and let it go wherever it would.

"Yes," Karen said. There was nothing in her tone or gaze that seemed insincere to Giselle.

"Giselle," Karen had said, her voice barely a whisper.

Giselle remembered all the things she had expected Karen to say next: she'd expected her to back out of the conversation entirely, brushing off her own worries as wedding jitters. She'd expected a vague, "My family has done things I'm not proud to be associated with"—the sort of sentiment that could leave Giselle fracking for specifics until it was time for the ceremony to start. And some part of her had dared to hope—or maybe dream—that Karen would go ahead and say, "My foolish aunt fell in love with Adolf Hitler," and be done with it.

She certainly hadn't expected what Karen actually said.

"Do you ever . . . do you ever feel apprehensive about befriending a German?"

Giselle had paused, her fingers tracing the intricate pattern of the lace tablecloth.

"Honestly, Karen . . ." she replied, then took a breath long enough to allow her a smear of reflective thought. "Sometimes I do. But I have to remind myself that I can't misjudge people based on their nationality. That's not who I am, and it's certainly not how I want my own people to be treated."

She had looked into Karen's eyes, searching for a flicker of understanding and shared humanity. She wasn't surprised when she found it.

"I feel the same way," Karen had confessed. "I don't want to be defined by my family's past. I want to be judged on my own merits, my own actions."

Giselle's heart had swelled with empathy. She had to admit that empathy, even extended to unlikely candidates, had come to her more easily in the wake of motherhood; but in that moment, she saw in Karen a kindred spirit. She was a young woman struggling to balance a past over which she'd had minimal control—with her present, her heritage, her aspirations.

"I don't judge anyone by their blood, Karen."

Giselle was certain that Karen would register the conviction in her voice; she heard it herself. Perhaps that was what infused her with the confidence to take the next gamble.

"If I've been . . . cagey around your family," she began, though she didn't think she had. Here was a moment of half-calculated vulnerability coming from both the real Giselle and the character she played around Karen. She continued, "it's not because of who you are, but because of what some of your family members might represent. And that's not entirely fair."

She took a deep breath and prepared herself to speak.

"I know that some Nazi families were given refuge in Argentina after the war."

Karen gasped, her eyes wide with shock and a flicker of fear. The word "Nazi" hung in the air.

What a loaded moment it had been. Giselle tried to deal with the impression that she'd unleashed a venomous snake between them that she couldn't put back in its cage—ruining everything, and the bigger—clearer—takeaway.

Giselle had turned her head away as though ashamed to have potentially offended her friend. It gave her time to breathe through the shock waves and find her baseline pulse again.

Giselle had seen something in Karen's eyes that had confirmed her suspicions—or more accurately, Felipe and Daniel's suspicions. It was a look of defiance, of rejection, of a young woman determined to break free from the shackles of her past. Giselle could have sworn she saw Karen's heart thudding out of her chest, the two of them sharing the same heartbeat. She could barely hear herself think over the whoosh of her own rushing blood. They had been right. They had been right about her.

It was at this moment that Giselle realized she needn't ride the fence of this tumultuous investigation anymore. As fraught as the moment was, this much, at least, was a great relief. So many times, she had tried to convince herself it couldn't be true—Karen didn't seem like someone who could be built of monster DNA. She was decent. She was the sort of woman a proud Jewess could have coffee with while their children giggled playing tennis side by side.

This was also the moment when Giselle realized she had begun considering the distinct possibility that all suspicions of Karen's terrible family history were true—and equally true was that Karen Fegel wanted nothing to do with Karen Fegelein.

Giselle reached out and took Karen's hand, her own trembling slightly.

"Karen," she whispered, "you need to trust me. Tell me everything. Maybe I can help you. I can certainly try."

The memory of that moment, the unspoken promise exchanged between two women from vastly different worlds, now echoed in Giselle's heart. She watched as Karen twirled across the dance floor, her laughter a melody bright enough to rival the orchestra's thumping tango. However, Giselle was acutely aware of an underlying darkness, a concealed secret poised to disrupt her delicate perception of happiness.

CHAPTER TWENTY-ONE

The harsh fluorescent lights of the hallway cast long, grotesque shadows on the walls, amplifying the chaos and confusion that reigned. Felipe slumped against the wall, each intake of his breath a ragged gasp. He watched helplessly as Daniel faced down their attackers. A crimson stain bloomed on the side of Felipe's shirt where the bullet had torn through his flesh.

Daniel, meanwhile, had no time to carefully weigh his options. He was outnumbered, outgunned, and his partner was bleeding out. The cold fury that ignited in his eyes spoke of a primal survival instinct that transcended fear. His lightning reflexes, on the other hand, were pure Mossad training.

Reaching into his pocket, Daniel flicked his Zippo lighter. He thrust it toward the ceiling, where he didn't simply let its flame tickle the nose of the fire alarm—he set the alarm's plastic cover on fire.

In seconds, the yellow-orange flame was hidden behind pluming black smoke.

The shrill wail of the alarm pierced the silence, shattering the tense standoff. Sprinklers along the hallway drenched the combatants in a cold, unrelenting shower. Then—just as Daniel had counted on—startled shouts and cries echoed through the hallway as elderly residents, clad in nightgowns and pajamas, emerged from their apartments, bleary-eyed, confused, and afraid.

The deluge proved enough to momentarily disorient the security guards, who lowered their weapons.

"Everyone back to your apartments!" one of the guards shouted, his voice barely audible above the din of the alarm. "These men are dangerous!"

Daniel saw his opportunity. He stood up but did not move away from Felipe's proned and bleeding figure.

"Listen to me!" he shouted, his Hebrew tinged with a thick American accent. "We're not here to harm you. We're here to capture a monster."

While this did nothing to alleviate the residents' confusion, their murmuring did quiet down. Daniel watched more than a few of them look at the armed security detail with some apprehension.

"We believe Adolf Hitler is living in this building," Daniel practically shouted. "He's had extensive plastic surgery and is hiding under a new identity."

A murmur of disbelief rippled through the crowd.

"That's impossible!" cried one woman whose sky-blue nightgown was patterned with brilliant Hawaiian flowers. "Israel is the last place Hitler would ever hide!"

"It's not true," Daniel insisted, ensuring, even in the pandemonium, to keep his tone empathetic. He reminded himself to imagine he was one of them, hearing for the first time that the enemy of the Jews had been his next-door neighbor for months, maybe years.

"He's here, among you," Daniel continued. "He knows what an unexpected hiding spot it is. He has family hiding in Buenos Aires, Argentina, and it is by investigating them that we learned enough to pinpoint his location. I understand it's difficult to believe, and there is ample evidence, but right now we are short on time. We need your help to find this evil and dangerous man."

He scanned the faces of the residents, searching for minor changes in their expressions that indicated their disbelief was shifting into cooperativeness. To his great relief, he saw those changes in face after face: eyes growing solemn, mouths settling into firm lines, chins titled upward in a way that indicated both willingness to listen and defiance against the man being discussed.

Daniel could not say he was surprised. This was what the Jewish community was left with. The Holocaust was a daily horror, a collective memory that many of them had to constantly reconcile with the reality around them. They were aware that a previous threat could return, and they did not ignore potential dangers by assuming everything was secure.

"If there's an older man in this building," Daniel continued, "a man named Otto who keeps to himself, who spends his days painting on his balcony . . . that man is Hitler."

A hush fell over the crowd, the only sound the steady drip of water from the sprinklers. Then, a frail voice spoke from the back of the group.

"Otto left yesterday," the voice said, its owner a stooped old woman with wispy white hair.

Daniel's body registered the statement before his mind did. His hands turned to lead mallets at his side. Sand filled his throat. His stomach froze over.

"Where did he go?" Daniel asked.

The old woman shrugged. "He didn't say, but he had a couple of suitcases with him. It looked like he was planning on being gone for a while."

Daniel and Felipe's eyes met, Felipe's still filled with fire despite his weakened physical state. The chilling realization forming in both their minds at once required no verbal communication.

In that instant, they knew.

Hitler was not in Tel Aviv. He was in Buenos Aires at Karen's wedding.

With Giselle.

CHAPTER TWENTY-TWO

T he flickering glow of the radio receiver illuminated Colonel Judd's weathered face as he listened intently to the faint crackle of music and laughter emanating from the speaker. The sounds of Karen's wedding reception—a joyous cacophony of tango rhythms and celebratory cheers—filled the cramped space.

Beside him, his team of retired Marines sat huddled around the monitoring equipment, their otherwise markedly different faces unified by the grim expression they all wore. Frank meticulously transcribed every word spoken into Giselle's wire, his pen scratching across the notepad with a rhythmic cadence. Miguel monitored the signal strength as his fingers danced across the dials with the precision of a concert pianist. Their stoic sniper, Hammerhead, kept a watchful eye on the hotel entrance, his rifle resting across his lap.

Judd, however, was not listening to the festivities. His mind was consumed by a growing sense of unease. He had been trying to reach Daniel for the past hour, but his calls went unanswered. He tried to tell himself it was nothing to worry about—his only means of talking to Daniel was calling the hotel room he shared with Felipe. He understood that if their own mission hadn't gone off with perfect timing and without a hitch, it could take quite some time for them to return. Yet, a cold knot of worry tightened in his gut. Had something gone wrong? Had Daniel and Felipe encountered trouble in Tel Aviv?

But it wasn't just Daniel's silence that troubled him. The way Giselle had abruptly turned off her wire earlier that day, claiming the need for privacy to call Felipe, struck him as odd under the circumstances.

Giselle was a seasoned operative, a woman of unwavering loyalty and impeccable judgment. She wouldn't risk jeopardizing the mission for a frivolous reason. The fact that she had chosen to silence her microphone just as Karen was on the verge of revealing crucial information had raised a red flag in Judd's mind. At the very least, he wanted to check in with Daniel and find out whether she had indeed called Felipe around the time she indicated. If not, there was no question that they had missed out on an exchange involving Karen.

He leaned forward with his eyes fixed on the receiver. The music from the ballroom swelled with sensual rhythms that awkwardly filled the van. Giselle's voice, however, remained conspicuously absent.

"Damn it," Judd muttered under his breath. "What is she up to?"

He hesitated, torn between his concern for her safety and his duty to the mission.

"Frank," he said, his voice gruff with worry. "Have you picked up anything significant from the reception?"

Frank shook his head without a glance up from his notes. "Nothing concrete, sir. Mostly small talk, congratulations, questions about the baby, that sort of thing."

He reassured Judd that they had taken down every name they'd heard mentioned, both earlier—when Karen and Giselle were working their way through the seating chart— and in current conversation, to make sure they caught any names missing from the guest list. He even tilted the notebook he was scrawling in so Judd could see the nature of his notes: beside one name, he'd written: "brought up a memory from when Karen was 5." Beside another name, he wrote: "calls himself her favorite uncle."

Judd sighed, his frustration mounting. This was what *so close yet so far* felt like—a raging headache that consumed his every thought.

"Miguel," he said, turning to his tech expert. "Any chance you can boost the signal? I want to hear everything, even whispers."

Miguel nodded, his fingers flying across the keyboard. The static on the receiver intensified, then cleared, revealing a clearer, crisper sound.

Judd leaned closer, straining to hear every nuance of the conversation. But still, Giselle remained silent.

He glanced at his watch. It was getting late. The reception would be winding down soon. If they were going to get any answers, they needed to act fast.

"I'm going to try to reach Daniel again," Judd muttered. "If I can't get through, we'll have to assume the worst."

He picked up the phone, his fingers dialing the familiar number. The line rang once, twice, three times. Then a click, followed by a recorded message in Spanish.

Judd's heart pounded in his chest, rivaling the volume of the phone receiver being slammed down.

"Damn it!" he exclaimed. "We've lost contact with them."

He turned to his team, his eyes hard and resolute.

"We need to find out what's happening in that ballroom," he said. "And we need to find out *now*."

CHAPTER TWENTY-THREE

The piercing wail of sirens echoed through the concrete canyons of Tel Aviv. When the ambulance pulled up to the curb outside, the apartment building reflected red and white lights. Paramedics' footsteps clattered on the marble flooring.

The residents—still reeling from the shock of both a fire alarm and the news that they'd been living among Adolf Hitler—shuffled back to their apartments with palpable reluctance.

Daniel knelt beside Felipe, his hands pressing against the wound, his eyes searching his friend's face for any sign of consciousness. Felipe's skin was clammy, his breathing shallow, labored. Daniel watched helplessly as Felipe's blood stained the pristine tile beneath him a deep, terrible red.

Felipe had to get to the hospital, and fast. But even as Daniel willed the paramedics to hurry, his mind raced toward yet another chilling realization. The security guards who had attacked them with the force and purpose of a militia were gone. They had vanished in the chaos. With a sickening certainty, Daniel knew where they were headed next: to warn Hitler that people had come for him.

The thought of Giselle, alone and vulnerable at Karen's wedding, sent a jolt of fear through him. He had to warn Judd to get her out of there before it was too late. And there was no time to hail a cab back to his hotel room or even ride with the ambulance and call Judd from the hospital.

Daniel's large fist hammered on the first apartment door to his right. Immediately, the door swung open to reveal a man who appeared to be in his seventies, wearing pajamas that looked several decades old. He peered up at Daniel through bloodshot eyes. He, like everyone on the floor, had witnessed so much that the sight of Daniel's hulking frame in his doorway didn't seem to alarm him at all.

"I need to use your phone," Daniel said by way of greeting.

In a box-sized kitchen that was either painted a dull brownish-yellow or had been stained that unfortunate color through extended exposure to nicotine, Daniel fumbled for the phone. His fingers were slick with his own sweat and Felipe's blood.

"Judd." Daniel's voice sounded raw, even to himself. "Felipe's been shot."

A beat of silence, then Judd's voice—concerned but sharp. "Is he alright?"

"He's alive," Daniel said. "The paramedics are coming for him."

"What happened? Where are you?"

"We found the building."

His words tumbled out fast. "But Hitler's gone. He left for Buenos Aires yesterday."

There was a sharp intake of breath on the other end of the line. "Here?" Judd echoed, unpacking the meaning of this news as Daniel explained.

"He's at Karen's wedding. With Giselle. And he's going by the name Otto Schwartz. *Otto Schwartz*," Daniel repeated with urgency. "You've got a live connection to her still, right? Let her know. Let her know right now, Judd."

Judd swore under his breath. A row of concerned, deeply concentrated faces swiveled toward him in the van. Judd stared at the monitoring equipment as if it held secret answers. His mental gears whirred as rapidly as a saw.

How? was the simple question running through his mind. *How did things go off the rails so quickly? How do I get her out of there safely? How? How? How?*

"I'll call you back from the hospital," Daniel promised.

"Judd, she needs to get out of there as quickly as possible. There's no doubt in my mind Hitler's goons have gotten word to him that we came sniffing around his apartment, and his hackles are going to be raised," Daniel added, knowing it was something Judd didn't need to hear but he needed to say.

"And he's going to wonder why someone was out to get him on the night of Karen's wedding," Judd said, half to himself and half for Daniel's benefit, in case he hadn't put two and two together in all the hubbub. "He's going to be looking for anyone outside the family who had firsthand knowledge of Karen's wedding."

Back in the hallway, a squad of paramedics crouched beside Felipe. As they assessed him, their bleak expressions unified them as much as their uniforms. Their movements were swift and efficient from years of habit-welding practice as they lifted him to the stretcher. Daniel followed them out of the building, his eyes scanning the surrounding streets for any sign of the missing guards.

Helpless to do anything else at the moment, Daniel issued a quick silent prayer.

"God," he let the word hang in the air for minute out of context, where it could have been either supplication or a curse.

He was thinking of how, in that moment, Felipe's blood was soaking through bandages on a stretcher and Giselle was wandering through the same closed-in space as Adolf Hitler. He was thinking of how he couldn't lose them—either of them, but certainly not both. Most of all, he was thinking of Elena. How it would feel to kneel down beside her and let her know that her parents weren't coming back home.

"Help Giselle and Felipe live," Daniel whispered into the inky black heavens. "Please."

CHAPTER TWENTY-FOUR

Giselle stood on the edge of the dance floor, watching as couples moved in rhythm to the lilting music of a small orchestra. The painful pinch of her stiletto heels was perhaps the only thing grounding her.

In the French neoclassical ballroom of the Hotel Alvear Palace, chandelier constellations lent a particular gleam to the gold leaf trim lining archways and columns. The air hummed not only with conversation, but also with the soft swish of what seemed like hundreds of satin and silk dresses. Porcelain place settings dotted impossibly white tablecloths. The scent of lilies, roses, and hydrangeas mingled with the faint sweetness of champagne and the delicate pastries stacked on silver platters.

The swirling beauty around her seemed almost too perfect, too serene, considering the truth that simmered just beneath the surface. She glanced around the room, her sharp eyes flicking from guest to guest. She wondered if *any* of them were innocent.

By any account, Karen had outdone herself. The bride stood in the center of the dance floor, radiant in her ivory gown. Her long brown hair, cascading in gentle waves, was pinned back by a glittering tiara. Her face was flushed with happiness as she twirled with her new husband, Hans, who beamed down at her with the easy smile of a man who believed he had won the greatest prize in the world. The two of them looked like something out of a fairytale—Karen's joy was so palpable that Giselle could almost forget why she was there. Almost.

She let her gaze slip past the newlyweds and land on the older woman sitting just a few tables away. Lotte was an imposing figure even as she sat still, her back ramrod straight, her hands resting primly in her lap. There was something steely in her gaze, something unyielding that belied the genteel exterior she so carefully presented. Giselle's mind drifted to the hours spent poring over old photos with Daniel and Felipe, noting the similarities between Lotte's sharp features and those of a younger Gretl Braun, Hitler's sister-in-law. If their suspicions were correct—and Giselle was almost certain they were—Lotte had once gone by a very different name.

Nearby, Nils Hoffman lingered at the edge of the ballroom, his tall, gangly frame blending in with the shadows. He was supposedly just Karen's cousin, but Giselle knew better by now. His involvement with far-right groups on campus had raised red flags from the start, leading Daniel, Felipe, and herself to scour through newspapers, searching for his name. His presence tonight was no coincidence; if anyone was likely to stir up trouble, it would be him. And yet . . . he seemed almost subdued, his eyes darting nervously around the room as if he were waiting for something—or someone.

Maybe, she thought to herself, *that someone is Otto Schwartz.* Moments before, Judd's voice sounded in her earpiece telling her, first, that Hitler was going by name Otto Schwartz, and second, that Daniel believed he was at this wedding reception tonight. When she'd heard it, she had numbly remembered Karen's "Uncle Otto" appearing on the guest list, and she was certain Judd's team had made note of the same.

Giselle felt a wave of unease settle over her. The room was too calm, too composed. Karen appeared overly content.

Karen.

Despite everything, Giselle couldn't suppress the small pang of warmth she felt toward the woman. Karen had always been kind to her, warmly and sincerely, despite the growing suspicions that shadowed their every interaction. She looked genuinely happy tonight—so beautiful and so unaware. Giselle wondered, not for the first time, how much Karen really knew. Was she just an unwitting pawn in a family web spun long before she was born, or was she a willing participant in the legacy of evil they were so close to uncovering? She would like to say their last interaction had cleared up more of her questions, but it really hadn't.

The memory of their earlier conversation—that raw honesty they had shared—tugged at her conscience once more.

Karen's voice, soft and vulnerable, echoed in Giselle's mind. "I'm so sorry, Giselle," she had whispered, her eyes glistening with unshed tears.

At the time, Giselle had interpreted Karen's apology as remorse for her family's past, for the atrocities they had committed. But now, in the harsh light of Judd's revelation, a different interpretation dawned on her.

Karen wasn't just sorry for her family's sins—she was sorry for her own complicity. She had known all along that Giselle was Jewish, yet she had continued to involve her in their gatherings, their secrets. Their lives.

A wave of anger washed over Giselle, a bitter taste rising in her throat.

How could Karen have exposed her to so many events in which the family she claimed to be unlike was gathered together, emboldening and shielding one another? Giselle had almost reached the point of feeling sorry for Karen—believing her innocent, unable to change the family she was born into. Innocently enjoying a wedding ceremony.

After reflecting on everything, a frost had quickly spread over her feelings toward Karen.

It wasn't like Karen *couldn't* sever her ties to them. She was an independent, working woman, now starting a new life for herself. And it was certainly true they were family—but at what point was that not enough? At what point did she have to confront the fact that her family had directly contributed to the murder of countless other families?

What would it take to wake a person up, to disenchant them from their family if that family's engineering of the Holocaust wouldn't do it?

Giselle's thoughts turned to Felipe, her husband, the love of her life. Recently, their relationship had become strained. In her loneliness and isolation, Giselle sought solace in her friendship with Karen, a connection that had blossomed into an unexpected bond.

But now, she looked around at Karen's guests and wondered which one of the old men there was the architect of her people's murders. Wondered if her sense of friendship with Karen had been little more than a crutch, a way to fill the void that had grown between her and Felipe. In the blindness born of her own need for companionship and understanding, she had allowed herself to become drawn into this family's sick, sick world.

~~~

Giselle's reverie was interrupted abruptly by a voice at her side.

"Care to dance?"

She turned to see a man standing beside her—medium height, a neatly combed head of gray hair, and a smile that didn't quite reach his eyes. He offered her his hand, his fingers slightly curled, inviting but commanding. There was a practiced charm to the way he held himself that immediately put Giselle on guard.

She hesitated, her instincts screaming against it. But she had a role to play, so she forced a smile and placed her hand in his.

"Yes," she said, letting him guide her to the dance floor. "Why not?"

The music shifted to a light, celebratory waltz, something distinctly Germanic. The man pulled her closer than she would have liked, his hand warm against her waist as they swayed together.

"I've heard," he said smoothly, his accent slightly clipped, "that you were a great help to Karen. She spoke highly of you— a friend during a difficult time, helping with the wedding, with her pregnancy."

Giselle smiled politely. "Karen is a lovely person. I was happy to help."

He nodded, his eyes sharp and assessing. "So, you are Giselle?"

"Yes," she replied simply, unsure of how much more she wanted to reveal.

There was something unnerving about the way his face lit up as if her name had struck a chord with him.

"Giselle. It's a beautiful name—French, no? Did you know it comes from the German word *geisil*?"

She looked at him, confused by the sudden change in tone.

"It means 'pledge,'" he continued, his voice softening into something almost reverent. "A lovely name . . . such depth in its origin. A name with purpose."

Giselle nodded, but her skin crawled under his gaze. There was something too dreamy in his expression, as if he was lost in a memory far removed from the present. She kept her expression cool, trying not to let her discomfort show.

It was then that a thought struck her—Judd's words, his somewhat frantic warning about Otto Schwartz. The man

206 • STEPHEN MAITLAND-LEWIS

they suspected to be Adolf Hitler in hiding. Her pulse quickened as she tried to keep her composure.

"Did I hear correctly," she asked casually, "that you're Karen's uncle Otto?"

The man blinked, then let out a soft laugh. "No, no, my dear. My name is Erwin Richter. Otto is over there."

He nodded toward an old man ambling about the ballroom with a camera, snapping pictures of the guests with a quiet, almost invisible presence. Giselle's heart lurched in her chest as her eyes locked onto the photographer. The verbal confirmation was one of the strongest pieces of evidence in their case thus far: *that* was Otto Schwartz. *That* was Adolf Hitler.

Erwin droned on about who he was in terms of the wedding—an old family friend who met Lotte at some event or another—something about his business ventures in door-to-door sales and his travels, but Giselle barely heard him. Her attention was fixed on the photographer, her mind racing with the implications.

The small camera embedded in her bracelet captured every detail, and the tiny earpiece in her ear buzzed faintly with the voices of the team stationed outside the hotel. Colonel Judd's voice cut through the haze, crisp and commanding.

"Giselle, we've got a clear shot of the photographer. Good work. Keep your distance and stay calm."

Giselle's heart pounded as she nodded imperceptibly. She let Erwin lead her through the rest of the dance, but her thoughts were miles away. When the music finally ended, she excused herself politely and moved toward the edge of the ballroom, her eyes never leaving the photographer. He was speaking now with a group of young people who had just entered the room, college-aged and clean-cut. The sort who may be reasonably expected to approach someone holding a camera at an event like this one and asked to have their picture taken. What she couldn't explain was the reverence in their expressions as they shook his hand, the deep bowing of their heads as though they truly wanted to bow at the waist but knew it would draw too much attention.

Except there was an explanation for it. The horror of that explanation was still catching up with her.

Giselle watched them closely, her stomach churning with suspicion. These weren't ordinary wedding guests. They were overly composed, especially for being Nils's age. Were they simply college friends of his, they might have been expected to stand in the corner, laughing a little too loudly and chugging wine meant to be sipped. But they were indeed his age and most feasibly guests of his—not Karen's.

Scanning their varying features and similar haircuts, she thought she spotted at least one face from the stack of photos Daniel had obtained from the foolish celebrity-chasing editor. She knew that had to be it: these were young men—and a couple of young women—from the same far-right campus group that that the three newspapers they visited were all investigating.

Throughout the night, Giselle had to keep grounding herself in little ways: taking deep breaths, shaking her head, clenching her hands tightly to be drawn back into her own body. Being surrounded by these revelers made for a blanketly bizarre experience already—and what she saw next was perhaps the most surreal moment that night. A split second after thinking of him for the first time in a while, she looked up and saw him.

Agustin Pérez—the editor of the young liberal newspaper she had visited during her investigation. He was standing near the entrance, looking around with a mixture of curiosity and apprehension.

Giselle weaved through the crowd until she was at his side.

"Agustin," she said softly, catching his attention.

He turned, his expression shifting from one of attentive observation to surprise. "What are you doing here?"

She gave him a small smile. "I could ask you the same thing, but I suspect I know the answer. You're here undercover—just like me."

His eyes widened slightly. "Undercover?"

"I'm not a journalist from Geneva," she said quietly. Then, with a deep breath, she added, "I am sorry I fooled you. I assure you I meant no harm and was—am—she corrected, very genuinely impressed by the work your paper is doing to expose what's happening under everyone's noses in Argentina. I am trying to do the same thing you are—end the new Nazi reign before it begins."

Agustin glanced around, his brow furrowing as he processed her words. "So . . . you're not here for the wedding?"

"Not exactly," Giselle replied. "I'm here because of Otto Schwartz—the photographer. I'm certain he's Adolf Hitler in hiding."

Agustin's expression darkened. "We've been hearing rumors that tonight was the night the new Nazi party would meet Hitler himself."

"That's right—you have a reporter infiltrating the meetings. Did he hear anything directly?"

"No. We have the impression only the top-ranking, most trusted group members were directly in the know on this one."

Giselle couldn't help being impressed by the clarity and command with which Agustin now spoke. Gone was the halting speech that exposed his nerves when he considered her simply as a lovely journalist there to flatter his ego.

He continued, "My reporter picked up enough to get the gist of time and place. Neither of us knew what I was even walking into before I got here."

Giselle nodded, her suspicions confirmed. "We're gathering evidence, and we've got a team outside ready to move when the time comes. But we could use your help."

Agustin's jaw tightened. "The police won't touch anything that smells like Nazi activity. I've tried."

"I know," Giselle said, something occurring to her just now. Something big. "Agustin, do you know the editors of many other papers around Buenos Aires well enough to call them personally?"

He nodded, brow rumpling.

"Would you? And tell them if they hurry, they can tell the story of Adolf Hitler getting arrested?"

Agustin continued nodding, more enthusiastically now but still with questions written across his forehead.

"That would go a long way toward waking Buenos Aires up to the Nazi threat, and it would get plenty high-ranking faces on permanent record . . . but how is he going to be arrested? Your team outside—do they have legal authority here?"

Giselle shook her head rapidly, as though answering him and dispensing the anxieties in her mind simultaneously. She was trying to think.

"They're doing reconnaissance and they're here in case things get ugly enough that I need an immediate rescue or Hitler tries to escape and needs to be detained—legally or not. But we'll figure out something. We have to."

Before Giselle could further brainstorm, Colonel Judd's voice crackled in her ear.

"Giselle. We're going to call in a bomb threat to the hotel. It'll get the police here, and once the media shows up, they'll have no choice but to act. They'll know that if they don't, they'll be exposed as the cowards who let Hitler walk."

Giselle's heart raced as she turned back to Agustin. "It's happening. We're going to get the police here. Can you make those calls?"

Agustin nodded with a neutral expression.

"Giselle," came Judd's voice again. "Things are about to happen fast. I want you tie up any loose ends you have,"—she knew he had to be thinking about her earlier conversation with Karen, the one he'd listened to all of except the very last moments—"and then leave. Don't run for it. Don't draw any attention. You and your newspaper buddy do what you have to do and get the hell out of there."

Speaking of those loose ends, Giselle spotted Karen across the room, still laughing with her husband—blissfully unaware of the storm poised to break. Giselle hesitated for a moment before making her way over.

"Karen," she said softly, catching the bride's attention.

Karen turned, her smile faltering slightly. "Giselle. What's wrong?"

Giselle glanced toward the group of young men gathered around the photographer. "Do you know who those people are? They're friends of Nils, right?"

Karen's expression stiffened almost imperceptibly. It took having known her and her expressions for months now, to detect that something was off.

"I suppose so. I didn't tell him he couldn't invite anyone to the reception. They're not causing any trouble, are they?"

"Not in terms of breaking wine bottles or hitting on the bridesmaids, no. But Karen . . . "

"But Karen what."

Her tone was abrupt enough to confirm, without other corresponding evidence, exactly what Giselle already knew.

"They're just kids at a party, Giselle."

Giselle narrowed her eyes. "Kids who were photographed with Nils when your mother had to threaten a newspaper not to run his picture."

Karen's face paled slightly. "I don't know what you think you know, but aren't you the one who said in our youth we all get photographed doing things that might embarrass us when we're older? These are *kids*," she doubled down on that point, practically spitting the final word into Giselle's face. "Kids go through harmless phases and then come out of them."

The word *harmless* rang in Giselle's ears, echoing the excuses she had heard before. She looked at Karen one last time, her heart heavy.

"Maybe," she said quietly. "Maybe not."

And with that, she turned away, leaving Karen to her perfect wedding, knowing that the world outside was about to come crashing in.

EPILOGUE

S unlight beamed through the bay windows of Daniel's
Geneva home, casting a warm glow over the picture
of domestic bliss unfolding within, a far cry from the
harrowing events of months past. A kaleidoscope of toys littered the Persian rug—a testament to the exuberant Elena.
Her laughter echoed through the room as she played Mousetrap with Daniel's twin sons.

The boys—teenagers now—towered over Elena, yet their
playful banter and shared giggles spoke of a bond that transcended age. One of the boys, his face alight with a mischievous grin,
nudged Elena. "Are you excited to be a big sister?" he asked, his
eyes twinkling.

Elena's face lit up, her smile radiant as she bounced on her
knees. "Yes, yes!" she squealed, her voice clear and confident.
"If it's a girl, I'm going to give her this game for a present."

"And if it's a boy?" Daniel's son questioned.

Elena scowled lightly. "Then I'm going to give *him* this
game for a present." Both twins, along with Giselle and Felipe,
laughed heartily at her reply.

Giselle and Felipe sat watching from the living room's
plush loveseat, their hands intertwined. The simple word
"present," articulated so perfectly by Elena, struck them as a
bittersweet milestone. So recently, it seemed, the little girl
had only been able to say "pwesent."

Their eyes met in silent conversation as Felipe gently
squeezed Giselle's hand, his thumb tracing soothing circles
on her skin. The warmth of his touch grounded her.

In the kitchen, the clinking of cups and the murmur of conversation provided a comforting soundtrack. Daniel and Claudia—Daniel's ex-wife—stood by the marble countertop, their interaction a far cry from the strained exchanges of the past. Time had refined their relationship, resulting in mutual respect and understanding.

With a warm and genuine smile, Claudia spoke of their sons' academic achievements, pride evident in every word. Daniel interspersed his own words of encouragement with his steady, listening nods. It was a scene that Giselle—not to mention the twin boys—had once believed to be impossible.

"I'm proud of you, Daniel," Claudia said, her voice soft, yet filled with conviction. "The work you're doing with the Red Cross, helping those children from the Paraguayan compound . . . it's truly inspiring."

Daniel's eyes further softened. Somewhere along the way, he had come to firmly believe he didn't have to keep his guard up with her anymore. "Thank you, Claudia. And I appreciate the wonderful job you've done raising our sons."

Their words hung in the air, a quiet acknowledgment of the shared journey they had undertaken: the mistakes made, the lessons learned.

Back in the living room, Giselle leaned closer to Felipe, her voice a hushed whisper. "How are you feeling, mi amor?" she asked, her gaze searching his. "About becoming a papa again?"

Felipe's grip on her hand tightened. He opened his mouth to answer, but the words seemed to catch in his throat.

She couldn't prevent her heart from pounding in her chest as she looked at him. The present moment was filled with a contentment she had not dared dream of only a short time ago. But still, she knew Felipe's scars ran deeper than the long-ago-sutured but still-tender wound in his side from being shot in Tel Aviv.

She knew that if everything had gone as planned with the takedown of Karen's nefarious family in Buenos Aires, she would have less reason to feel apprehensive as she looked up at her husband, searching his face for any sign of how he felt about the upcoming birth of their second child. But nothing had gone as planned.

The memory of sitting with Felipe in the hospital when they found out felt like a fresh gut punch.

The fluorescent lights of the Tel Aviv hospital had cast a harsh, clinical glow, and the air hung heavy with the sharp scent of disinfectant—both constant reminders of the sterile world they were stuck in—this visit, and Felipe's, just a short time before.

Giselle sat by Felipe's bedside, her hand clasped tightly in his. His face, still pale from the gunshot wound, bore the lines of exhaustion and pain. Daniel paced the room restlessly, his brow furrowed in concentration as he read and reread and reread the newspaper article:

Local Vigilantes Lead Police to Arrest Innocent Man

By Gael Fernandez, Editor, *El Sensacional*

In a stunning display of incompetence and deceit, local law enforcement were led astray by a band of self-proclaimed vigilantes, resulting in the arrest of an innocent man during a fabricated bomb scare at the prestigious Hotel Alvear Palace. The police responded to a reported bomb threat, only to find there was no bomb, but rather a tangled web of lies spun by a rogue ex-Mossad agent and his associates.

Daniel Lavy—formerly of Israel's Mossad before being ousted in disgrace—along with his supposed "investigators," misled authorities into arresting an elderly photographer whom they claimed was Adolf Hitler himself, hiding under the name Otto Schwartz. This man was neither Adolf Hitler nor Otto Schwartz.

In fact, this innocent man was simply a photographer whose name remains unknown. The real identity of "Otto Schwartz" is now in question, as it appears to have been nothing more than an elaborate fabrication designed to thrust Lavy and his crew into the limelight, perhaps in a desperate attempt to restore the reputation he lost when Mossad kicked him to the curb.

It should be noted that Daniel Lavy has a sordid history of deception, having stolen photographs from this very newspaper in the past. The reality is, no one can even confirm the existence of this "Otto Schwartz," let alone prove he is Hitler.

The actions of Lavy and his accomplices have only served to embarrass our city's police force and cast doubt on legitimate investigations. While they claim to be fighting evil, what they have done is arrest an innocent man based on lies, only to have it blow up in their faces when their supposed "evidence" crumbled under the weight of reality.

It's time to ask: How much longer will we tolerate these vigilantes running amok, feeding the public their fantasies and tarnishing the reputations of real investigators?

~~~

The sound of Daniel Lavy's boots echoed sharply across the small hospital room, his pacing relentless, fueled by a storm of anger.

"*Innocent* man," he growled, tossing the crumpled copy of *El Sensacional* onto the bedside table with a scowl. "How dare they call him 'innocent.'"

Felipe, half-sitting in the hospital bed and somewhat woozy from pain medication, winced as he shifted to look at the paper. His voice was faint without sounding weak—his frustration lent his voice a certain edge even in his current state. "They didn't even mention Lotte or Nils getting arrested. They twisted everything."

Giselle, perched on the windowsill, crossed her arms as she scanned the article, her expression unreadable. "Of course they did," she said calmly. "It's *El Sensacional*. They thrive on sensationalizing the truth."

Daniel slammed his fist on the side of the bed, his face flushed with rage. "They've made me look like a fool! Made all of us look like fools! 'Innocent man,' my ass! That 'innocent' man was Heinrich Hoffmann, Nazi propagandist, for God's sake! He's responsible for some of the vilest images and lies spread by that regime."

Giselle nodded quietly. "But they don't care about that. They only care about the spectacle."

Felipe exhaled, sinking back against his pillows, the weight of the world in his eyes. "So, Hoffmann wasn't Otto Schwartz. He was still a Nazi," he murmured. "That much is true. He admitted it when they had him in custody. But . . ." He trailed off, his voice pained. "Hitler was there, wasn't he? Right in front of us, and we missed him."

Giselle's face tightened as she recalled the night at the hotel. She danced with him. Erwin, he had called himself—so smooth, so confident. She had felt it then, that unsettling feeling in the pit of her stomach. And now it all made sense. He had been the one to point to the wedding photographer—in reality Heinrich Hoffmann as Otto Schwartz—so her attention, and her team's attention, would redirect to him.

Heinrich himself had confirmed it for them. He'd been angry enough upon finding out he'd been set up to take the fall meant for Hitler, that his cooperation seemed like a possibility. He was offered a deal: his son, Nils, had been arrested on conspiracy to commit domestic terrorism. He would spend years of his life in jail for his "harmless" youthful indiscretions. So, Heinrich was offered the chance to ensure the boy's freedom in exchange for evidence of the real identity of Adolf Hitler.

At that point, Heinrich had turned over all his photographs of Hitler taken over the years. It seemed he had continued on as the ignoble leader's official photographer even in hiding, which meant he had pictures of Hitler's new face. It had already occurred to Giselle that the man who'd misdirected her toward Heinrich was likely to blame, but now she could see it for herself. She could look at photograph after photograph of the slimy man she had danced with, chest to chest.

When his goons from Tel Aviv had contacted him about the break-in and attempt to find him, he must have realized that meant that whoever was investigating him would already know he'd been living under the name Otto Schwartz. He must have confirmed he was dancing with the enemy when Giselle casually asked if he was Karen's uncle Otto. He must have spent all night making sure Nils's young college friends were sent over to Heinrich Hoffmann. While they thought they were meeting the Fuhrer himself, Heinrich thought he was simply meeting his son's school friends. He was probably moved by the young men's somber and respectful nature.

With Giselle's attention firmly directed toward Heinrich Hoffmann, the real Adolf Hitler had been free to slip away quietly.

In the hospital, the room became silent, with everyone aware of the unsuccessful result. Felipe stared at the ceiling, his face pale with pain and exhaustion. "So what now?" he asked quietly. "We've been burned in the press. Nils is out there. And Hitler . . . he's already vanished again."

For a long moment, no one spoke. The only sound was the faint beeping of the heart monitor beside Felipe's bed and the distant hum of hospital activity.

Giselle slowly straightened her back and stood from the windowsill. "We keep going," she said firmly. "We may have taken a hit, but it's not over. Not even close."

Daniel looked at her, his eyes still simmering with anger, but something softened in his expression. "We're not exactly in a good position here, Giselle."

"I know," she admitted. "But we've brought down Heinrich Hoffmann and Gretl Braun. We have all of Hoffmann's photographs, and we have his cooperation. That's a major victory. And we have Agustin Perez on our side now—a true soldier in this fight. He's not going to let the truth stay buried."

Felipe glanced at her, his eyes tired but searching. "Do you really think we still have a chance?"

"I do," Giselle said, her voice resolute. "Hitler may have slipped away this time, but we're closer than ever. He'll change his alias, but we'll learn the new one like we learned this one. We know who he's working with. And we've taken out two key players in his network. We just need to regroup, gather our strength, and hit him harder next time. Agustin will help us expose the truth. We'll have another shot."

The room fell silent again, but this time, the mood was different—less somber, more determined. Giselle's words hung in the air, a promise of hope amid the darkness.

Now, in Daniel's living room—surrounded by family as sunlight painted dappled patterns on his antique furnishings—they all occupied this tableau of perfect domestic harmony. Elena's infectious giggles filled the air as she played with Daniel's sons, the colorful Mousetrap game a centerpiece of their shared amusement.

The warmth of Felipe's touch and the gentle rise and fall of his chest as he breathed anchored Giselle in the present, muting the memory of how learning Heinrich Hoffmann's true identity had initially devastated them. The realization that they had not captured Hitler, only his loyal accomplice, had once felt like such a crushing blow. But looking up at her husband's now-serene face, Giselle was able to look at the situation positively.

The realization had been a double-edged sword. It brought a renewed sense of urgency—a determination to track down the elusive monster. But now they knew what he looked like. And now they knew so much more about his strategies than they ever had before.

Felipe's eyes met his wife's, his gaze filled with a depth of emotion she had rarely seen before. The events of the past months had stripped away the layers of cynicism and left behind a raw vulnerability.

"Giselle," he began, his voice thick with emotion.

His thoughts were interrupted by Claudia, who approached them with an envelope in hand. "Are you still having your mail forwarded from Buenos Aires?" she asked.

"Yes, for now," Giselle replied, taking the envelope. "We're not in any hurry to return." The events in Buenos Aires had left a bitter taste in their mouths, a lingering unease that made the prospect of returning unbearable.

Aside from the disappointment of not catching Hitler and their names being dragged through the mud, Giselle couldn't shake the image of Karen just standing there—less than an hour after her wedding—watching her mother, a boy she called her cousin, and several others being arrested. The memory of her happy day would be subsumed by the darker memory of losing her family and being betrayed by the woman she once called her best friend. Giselle could distinctly recall watching Karen's face go ashen and her expression turn into a mask of horror.

Claudia nodded in understanding. "This came for you," she said, handing Giselle the envelope. "I don't recognize the return address."

Giselle's heart skipped a beat as she saw the name on the envelope: Karen Fegelein. A chill ran down her spine as she carefully opened the letter, her fingers trembling slightly.

Inside, a single sheet of paper bore Karen's elegant script.

Giselle,

I hope this letter finds you well. It has been a difficult few months since the . . . events at my wedding. I have been navigating this pregnancy and the early days of my marriage without my mother by my side. But I have found solace and support in my dear Aunt Romilda. You may know her by another name.

Giselle gasped, the letter slipping from her grasp. Aunt Romilda. The name echoed in her mind, a chilling realization dawning upon her. Romilda Lehmann, the mysterious owner of the penthouse apartment where Lotte and Nils had resided. The woman they had suspected of being a key player in the Nazi network but had never been able to identify.

Could it be? Was Karen's Aunt Romilda, in fact, Eva Braun? The woman who had proudly carved an identity for herself as Hitler's wife, living under an assumed identity?

From where he sat, Felipe observed that his wife's breathing had increased and her brow had become mopped with sweat, but he couldn't see the words on the stationery nor the name on the envelope. "What's going on, Giselle?" he asked.

She looked at him. She was still waiting for him to answer her—to tell her how, indeed, he felt now as he thought of becoming a papa again. She knew she couldn't delay sharing the content of the letter with him for long: he and Daniel both needed to understand that a dam had broken inside Karen on the night of her wedding—and that whatever progress they'd made against the Hitler clan, they had gained a new, potentially formidable, enemy.

But first, before she could bring herself to share the news, she needed to hear what Felipe had to say. With her heart threatening to beat its way out of her chest, she folded the letter in half so that Karen's elegant but angry handwriting was hidden.

"Please," Giselle said quietly, "first tell me what you were going to say. To the question I asked you."

He paused, his gaze drifting toward Elena and the boys, their laughter a symphony of innocence and joy. "The world can be a cruel place," he continued, his voice barely a whisper. "I've seen its darkness firsthand. And the thought of bringing another child into such a world . . . it terrified me."

Giselle nodded, understanding the weight of his words. The fear, the uncertainty, the desire to protect their loved ones from the horrors they had witnessed—she felt it all too. She hardly knew what to do with it sometimes, and growing attached to Karen Fegelein had hardly helped her make sense of her tumultuous emotions.

Felipe took a deep breath, his eyes locking onto hers. "But then I realized something," he said, his voice gaining strength. "We can't let fear dictate our lives. We can't let the darkness win."

He reached out, his hand cupping her cheek, his thumb gently tracing the curve of her lips. "We have something to offer our child, Giselle," he said with a quiet conviction. "We can give them love, and hope, and a family who will fight for them, no matter what."

The fear that had gnawed at her heart began to dissipate. In its place was a growing sense of warmth that felt much more stable than the heady blips she had grown accustomed to relying on throughout their latest investigation of Hitler.

"Yes," she whispered, her eyes glistening with tears. "We can."

Felipe's smile was a beacon of light, a promise of a future filled with love and resilience. "I'm excited about the baby, my love," he said. "More excited than you can imagine."

In that moment, as the sunlight danced on the walls and the laughter of children filled the air, a sense of peace settled over them. The world may still hold its monsters, its shadows of the past, but they had found—if not in the world, then within themselves—a sense of haven and sanctuary that was untouchable.

The battle was far from over, but they would face it together, hand in hand—their hearts filled with the unwavering belief that in the end, love would always triumph over darkness.

ABOUT THE AUTHOR

photo credit: Darien Photographic

Stephen Maitland-Lewis is an award-winning author, British attorney, and former international investment banker whose career has spanned London, Kuwait, Paris, Munich, and Wall Street.

After relocating to California in 1991, he ventured into hospitality and media as the owner of a luxury hotel, a celebrated restaurant, and Director of Marketing for a Los Angeles daily newspaper.

A lifelong jazz aficionado, he serves as a Board Trustee of the Louis Armstrong House Museum in New York and received the Museum's prestigious Louie Award in 2014. Maitland-Lewis is also a Freeman of the City of London and

225

a member of PEN, The Authors Guild, the International Mystery Writers Festival, and the California Jazz Foundation.

His acclaimed novels include *Legacy of Atonement*, *Hero on Three Continents*, *Emeralds Never Fade*, *Ambition*, *Botticelli's Bastard*, and *Duped*. His short fiction collection, *Mr. Simpson and Other Short Stories*, features the award-winning title story, later adapted for the stage.

He divides his time between Rancho Mirage, California, and New Orleans, Louisiana.